The God-Fearer

THE TRAP
A DANCE IN THE SUN
THE PRICE OF DIAMONDS
THE EVIDENCE OF LOVE
THE BEGINNERS
THE RAPE OF TAMAR
THE WONDER WORKER
BEGGAR MY NEIGHBOUR AND OTHER STORIES
THE CONFESSIONS OF JOSEF BAISZ
HER STORY
ADULT PLEASURES
HIDDEN IN THE HEART

The God-Fearer

A NOVEL BY

Dan Jacobson

Charles Scribner's Sons
New York

Maxwell Macmillan International
New York Oxford Singapore Sydney

Copyright © 1992 by Dan Jacobson

Charles Scribner's Sons
Macmillan Publishing Company
866 Third Avenue
New York, NY 10022

Macmillan Publishing Company is part of the Maxwell Communication Group of Companies.

Library of Congress Cataloging-in-Publication Data
Jacobson, Dan.
The God-fearer: a novel/by Dan Jacobson.
p.   cm.

ISBN 0-684-19660-3
I. Title.
PR9369.3.J3G63   1993
823'.912—dc20   93-7525   CIP

10 9 8 7 6 5 4 3 2 1

Printed in the United States of America

As a man might dream of hurt he has received,
And, dreaming, wish that it were a dream.

Dante: *Inferno*, Canto XXX

The God-Fearer

ONE

His name was Kobus the Bookbinder. His whole life, aside from the period of his apprenticeship and early manhood, had been spent in a small town called Niedering. It lay in the most westerly region of the land of Ashkenaz.

When asked how old he was Kobus invariably replied: eighty-four. That was as good a guess as he could make. Dealing with numbers of any kind had long been difficult for him. It was impossible for him to recollect even the date attached to the current year, let alone the year of his birth. The one fact about both dates which was fixed in his mind was that each in its turn supposedly gave the sum of years that had passed since the very day on which God had created the universe.

What a story! Kobus did not believe it for a moment. It amazed him that anyone, the wisest or most self-confident of scholars included, should have had the impudence to imagine that he actually knew when the world had been created, or by whom, or for what purpose.

As with much else, Kobus kept his scepticism on this subject to himself.

By trade he had been what his cognomen suggested: a master printer and bookbinder. His achievements as a craftsman had at one time been known and respected all over his own part of the country and beyond. Together with a few journeymen and apprentices and some unskilled hands, he used to do jobbing printwork and binding of all kinds. He produced religious works in the sacred tongue, and tales of travel, poetry, medical books, and histories in our secular language. But the printshop and his stock had been sold a long time before. Neither of his sons nor his son-in-law had wished to follow him in the trade, and eventually he found it too burdensome to continue the business on his own.

His elder son had married the daughter of a landowner nearby and soon grew to look down on his father, the tradesman; the other son, the one whom Kobus had trained and favoured and nourished high hopes for, had left home to become a soldier under Manasse, the self-styled Sar of the Upperland, and nothing more had since been heard of him. Kobus's only daughter married a teacher in Niedering, a learned man in his own uninspired fashion, but quite impractical, useless as a potential successor in the printing business. His hands were plump and soft and pale, but in his father-in-law's eyes they had about as much adroitness as a pair of little trowels.

Enough of that. When he sold the house and workshop, which were on the outskirts of Niedering, Kobus and his wife Rahella moved into a smaller place: one big room downstairs, two rooms above, a yard at the back. They had thought it safer and more comfortable to be there, in a little street with neighbours nearby and the marketplace just a few minutes away. Naturally he missed (and especially at first) the space they had had before, and the orchard in front of the old house. Much to his surprise he found that he did not miss the work at all.

Rahella died about two years after they had made the move. She had been ailing and querulous for a long time before her death, which, Kobus had to confess inwardly, came as something of a relief to him. It may even have done the same for her, though he could not guess what she actually felt at the very end. By then she had fallen silent; her spells of apparent wakefulness had become as wordless as the ever-extending periods of unconsciousness into which she was constantly lapsing.

It would have been comforting for him to believe that she was resigned to her going. But for all he knew her silence may have been one of terror.

Even before the death of his wife, Kobus's own existence had seemed to him not much more than a kind of postscript to a life that was already concluded. Once Rahella had gone, that feeling inevitably became even stronger than before. As a man grows older – at any rate this had been his experience – it becomes more and more difficult for him to find good reasons for carrying on, quite simply. In earlier years, even when his children were quite adult, he had been able to tell himself that they still needed him, or to ask himself what would become of the business if he were to leave the scene. But now? After Rahella's death? He could no longer even say to himself, 'Well, Rahella needs me.'

His children, he knew, thought of him chiefly as a source of guilt and misgiving. (Except for the soldier, of course, who, if he was still alive, presumably thought of him not at all.) Kobus did not have any complaints against the two who were still living nearby; not at all. Both of them, in their different ways, wished to do more for him than they could, or than he would let them; they also wished that they had to do less for him than they did; then they reproached themselves for both sets of wishes. To his grandchildren, even the grown-up ones, he was a kindly stranger, hardly more: the gulf between the years he had lived and the years they still had to live was too great for either side to bridge. How could they really believe that one day they would be as old and shrivelled and bent as he was? And they were quite right to find the thought incredible, since (should they live long enough) they would then indeed no longer be the people they were when their grandfather had been alive.

As for his two tiny great-grandchildren: to them, so far as they were conscious of him at all, he surely made a bizarre and perhaps even frightening spectacle. A ten-year-old was in their eyes virtually an adult: what kind of creature, then, did they make him out to be?

All that was clear and coherent enough in his mind.

Though sometimes Kobus was not sure that his wife's name really had been Rahella. That was the name recollection offered him, the name his pen inscribed, without hesitation, with the same speed and self-assurance with which it produced any other word, when he sat at his desk, as he often did, trying to put his thoughts in order. But once the name stood there on the page, fixed, as if waiting for him to look at it, it seemed unfamiliar, even slightly menacing, difficult to associate with the silently breathing shape under the bedclothes which he had found, one morning, to be breathing no longer. 'Rahella! Rahella!' Is that what he had cried at it? At her? Is that what he said over and over again as he took her hand in his own and looked at the grey wasted face turned to one side on the pillow, with its eyes irrevocably closed? If so, why did he have no memory of the syllables on his tongue? If not, what name did she carry all the years that had gone before?

Well, setting that aside, he remained fairly sure

of everything else: his name, and the name of the town he lived in, and his widowed state, and the fact that he had had three children who survived their childhood, and that he had five or possibly six grandchildren and definitely two great-grandchildren.

The real confusions in his mind began later; or began elsewhere. He could never separate the confusion that seemed to inhere in certain events from the confusions of his attempts to recollect them. He knew that an 'accident' had befallen him; but what form this accident had taken, how it happened, even when it happened – all that remained a mystery to him. He was told afterwards that he had been found on the floor, in the room downstairs, near the door to the street. How long was it after the accident that he had been found there? Nobody knew. He was unconscious. There was a gash on his forehead.

Later, when he put his hand to his brow, well above the left eye, he could touch the scar with his fingertips. Faintly tender still, it felt like a hard worm, if such an object could be imagined. What had produced it? Had he suffered an apoplexy of some kind, and cut his head in falling? Or had he merely stumbled over something? Or perhaps fought off an intruder?

Any guess was as good as any other. He had no recollection whatever of the mishap. Even the period after he had returned (more or less) to consciousness remained with him subsequently as a blur, for the most part. He remembered of it random noise; too much light; too much darkness; the presence of many strangers, or rather of people who claimed an intimacy with him he could not understand; something remorseless going on outside him and something feeble going on inside him. And of course the hideous cuppings and leechings to which he had been subjected, together with the evil-smelling and even fouler-tasting concoctions which he was compelled to swallow.

All these experiences ran promiscuously into one another and then departed, as if in a hurry, like a routed army, leaving him more or less where he had been. Recovered – ostensibly. In silence. Frailer than before. Even more distant from himself. Even more dependent than before on the ministrations of Elisabet.

Housekeeper, cook, cleaner, butt, object of pity and scorn, Elisabet was somewhat younger than her master but even less prepossessing. At least, Kobus hoped he was not deluding himself on that score. She was skinny but big-bottomed; splay-legged; bent forward at the hips and bent upwards at the neck. Denied a bridge to her nose, she had been endowed by way of compensation with exceptionally narrow, deep nostrils. The upward twist of her neck made it all the easier for the onlooker to gaze into these; as well as to take note of the limited yet exaggerated range of expressions which crossed her little face.

There was her scowl of unavailing concentration; her puffed-cheek, closed-eye acknowledgement of pain; her rare grin of pleasure, when both her elongated yellow teeth were revealed; her generalised wrinkling up from chin to forehead, which showed that respect and wonder were going on within. All these expressions were accompanied by more or less identical gasps. She spoke little, and when she did it was difficult to follow her. Her clothes were rags. Her smell was not sweet.

But Kobus was not really in a position to belittle her. (Though he did it of course; sometimes in his mind, occasionally with his pen, most often with his tongue, when she irritated him sufficiently.) She was the only person on earth to whom he remained a figure of power, even if one diminished from what he once had been. He could read, he could write, he owned many books, he had three rooms to himself, he had a son and a daughter to protect him, he had money and valuables concealed in a strong-box (she did not, he believed, know where under the floorboards it was concealed) and more money still deposited with the local Hanaper. Whereas she existed on sufferance in the hovel of her daughter and son-in-law. A paviour by trade, the latter used his fists on her, and on the daughter, and on his children too, whenever he felt particularly aggrieved about the disappointments life had brought him. Kobus had seen the marks on her.

What Elisabet longed for most in the world was for him to offer her a permanent place under his roof. No, not as his wife or mistress (her ambitions were not that elevated; and anyway she must have had a pretty good idea of his current capacities in that direction). It was promotion to the role of resident housekeeper for which she longed. So far he had not extended the invitation to her. Only when he had been confined to bed after the accident was she allowed to remain there constantly; once he had got up he banished her again. For days thereafter she went about her cooking and cleaning and other such tasks with a fierce look of injury fixed on her preposterous little face.

Bit by bit, as best he could, and with Elisabet's help, Kobus began to put together again the modest domesticities that had sustained him before the accident. He got up in the morning, ate the dishes she prepared for him, walked (a little), opened the shutters and stared out at the life (not very much of it) that passed in the street. There were plaster and lath houses like his own across the road, with tiled roofs and twisted chimney-pots; a bakery; an old woman who sold, directly from her doorway, cabbages and other greens (fresh in summer, pickled in winter) and sometimes more exotic fruits like oranges, figs, pomegranates. Though the town was considered to be quite large, farmyard as well as human smells were never far from his nostrils. There were dogs to be seen; small windows, some of them leaded and glazed, like the one Kobus looked out of; dim lights flickering here and there after dusk – that kind of thing. Occasionally he would visit his son who would bring him back in his 'carriage', as the son loved to call it, though to Kobus's eyes it was little more than a pony-trap. More often he would go to his daughter's for a meal. If time seemed to go by even more slowly than it had in the past, if he felt both more indifferent to himself and the world outside him, and yet always conscious of the sadness of the past, of the present, of the future he would never know – well, that too was merely an intensification of states long familiar to him. Stark or subdued dawns came up at his bedroom window; summer afternoons expanded as if they would never end and then contracted meekly, as they had to, into dusk; night produced its usual effects of faint gleams and isolated footsteps, sleep and wakefulness.

That he could hardly tell the events of the days apart from one another, even while he was going through them, did not worry him greatly. What he found himself incessantly puzzling over was something more trivial. Or so an outsider might have thought. It was the fact that he simply could not remember the *names* of those indistinguishable days. The Sabbath day was easy, and so was the Sabbath eve, when the whole town was hushed, and the town-guard wore their finery, or what passed as such among them, and men and boys in their best clothes could be seen going about the streets, on their way to and from the town's two places of worship. So that was the Sabbath: easy. But the next day? What was it *called*? And the day after that? Nothing should have been plainer; but in fact nothing proved more obscure to him – until the Sabbath eve would come round again, sometimes sooner than Kobus had expected it to, sometimes later.

The same problem arose with much else besides the names of days. All sorts of words, which had once seemed as firmly attached to particular things as his own name was to him, had drifted loose and would not be tethered down again. For instance, he might find himself turning over a spoon in his hand and wondering what it was called; on more than one occasion he even gazed in the same bemused fashion at his own fingers. Other appellations came readily enough, but seemed peculiarly indocile once they had arrived; they had a will of their own and led him into unfamiliar places. As with Rahella's name, they sounded strange in his own head; they made unconvincing shapes and patterns when he tried to write them down.

Ashkenaz. That was another case in point. It

was, he was usually convinced, where he lived, where he had always lived; where his grandparents and (as far as he knew) their grandparents had lived; and yet, having written the word down, he would find himself staring at it as if it were the name of some foreign part he had never seen. Ashkenaz . . . Ashkenaz . . . Perhaps in the end it was nothing more than one of those mythical countries, supposedly visited by travellers of times long past, which he had read about in the books he had once made a habit of collecting. How could he tell?

There were many similar instances. When people repeated rumours about great public events (that the Muselmi had tried to put an army into the land of Pannonia and had been driven back with much loss of life; that the so-called Davidic Chief Priest of Yerusalaim had been taken prisoner by the Farasim, who had appointed their own candidate, an upstart Ectabani, in his place) he would sometimes nod wisely, as if the references they made were familiar to him. But they were not. Occasionally, in speaking to his son and daughter-in-law, he would see them exchange glances with one another: half-amused and half-alarmed. Then he would try to remember what word he had just used that might have provoked them to exchange such a look. Better, he would think, to have said something like, 'I can't remember the name,' or, 'What's it called,' or, 'Thing . . . thing,' than to have made a mincemeat of his own speech. But no, these words, whatever they were, would just fly off his tongue; apparently so right, and yet apparently so wrong.

Reading was another difficulty. He used to be a great reader. It went with the trade, he would say, by way of excuse. (Actually this was an untruth; some of the most skilled among his colleagues and competitors had been quite indifferent to the contents of what they dignified or even ennobled with their art.) He used to read all sorts of books, though never the Holy Scriptures which he had been compelled to study as a lad; nor the commentaries on these, and the commentaries which had proliferated on the commentaries. Other kinds of writing had seized his imagination – legends, histories (or what purported to be histories); above all, those travellers' tales about the sights they claimed to have seen in distant corners of the world. With them he had travelled to the land of Sinn, where the great teacher Buddh does not rule but waits eternally for men to follow him; to Hoddo, where they worship gods that have many arms and heads, many organs and many orifices to put them into; to Habbash, whence the Queen of Sheba had set out to pay tribute to the King Solomon and gone home again with his child and his Law; to regions more remote still, where, it was said, even the Christer people had their own kings and queens; to places more fantastical than these. From such books he had become acquainted with amazing beasts, stones that spoke, rivers that flowed uphill, great cities of crystal, kingdoms without end, a copper-skinned people inhabiting a giant, unvisited continent far in the west . . .

Of all of these he had read in several languages: in the sacred tongue, in Ashkenazit, Spharadit, Latinit.

Oh yes, he had passed for a scholar, in this town at least, once upon a time.

Now he could read nothing. His eyes could no longer focus on a single line of type; not even in the narrowest of columns. His gaze constantly jumped above or below the line he was trying to read, turning everything into rubbish.

This was a further deprivation, of course. But if he were to admit the truth to himself, it was more like a deprivation remembered than felt as a present loss. It was, in the end, just another aspect of the emptiness he occupied, and which occupied him.

Into this emptiness, eventually, there came a change.

Somewhere within his mind, as if at the very corners of his brain, he became aware of movements and shifts, changes of pressure, flurries, cracks, creaks, small but decisive liftings and sinkings, as of animals stirring, or of tiles or timbers settling. What made all these nudges and

14

tamperings more disturbing to him was precisely the fact that they seemed to be taking place not only inside his head, but also outside him, in the very fabric of the house he lived in.

Everyone who lives in solitude knows the feeling that (a) he is not alone; and (b) whatever is keeping him company is determined for its own reasons to elude him. Or rather determined both to elude him and to let him know that it is there.

So it was with him, or with whatever it was now intruding on him. Just when he wasn't looking, just when he wasn't listening, when his attention was diverted – it was then that apprehensions of this kind came to him. Quite sharp and clear, they were; and yet for all his vigilance, they always took him by surprise; he was always too late to catch the exact moment when they occurred.

Something or someone had been watching him, and he had not known it was doing so until it was gone. A noise he had not been aware of was no longer audible; its cessation alone told him that he had missed it. Had not that door been closed when he had last looked at it? Surely that shutter or drape now hanging so still, so demurely still, had swelled forward and fallen back just a moment before. Hadn't it?

That's how it was.

Until, on an evening indistinguishable to his senses from any other, the source of the unease he

15

had been feeling chose to make itself known.

There they were at last, made visible in front of him: the secret co-tenants of his living space.

A more innocent spectacle it would have been difficult to imagine.

It was a puzzle to Kobus, later, that he should never have doubted for a moment the connection between his visitors and all the starts and stirrings that had gone before. It was as if, from deep within a turmoil of fear and dismay, he wanted to say, 'Oh, so it was you all the time. Now I know.'

In the middle of the downstairs room, kneeling on the floor, their heads together, apparently engrossed in a game they were playing and which Kobus could not see, were two children, a boy and a girl. The girl was a year or two older, he would have guessed, than the boy. She must have been about nine years old. She was wearing a long, velvety dress, spotted with white flowers. The hem of it was spread copiously on the floor around her. The boy wore trousers and a sleeveless red jerkin; of wool, Kobus supposed. There was nothing misty or unclear about them. Kobus could see the freckles on the boy's ingenuous, chubby face; he could see the tips of the girl's little ears peeping through her hair, which hung down almost to her shoulders. She wore a small, white, close-fitting embroidered cap which was tied with ribbons beneath her chin;

16

and her hair, which was straight and dark, seemed to spring out below the cap, as if to escape from the constraint of it. The boy's head was bare.

Their lips moved, the kneeling boy sat back on his heels, gazing downwards, the girl crouched lower over the floor, and not a sound came from them. Neither of them took the slightest notice of Kobus. He stood in the doorway, transfixed, unable to speak or to advance on them, or even to shut his eyes and so hide them from his gaze, or himself from them. All he could do was to stare. And to feel his heart banging away, as if it hung inside some empty space much larger than his breast.

Later they were gone. He did not know how much later. He did not know where they went, or how they went. He simply discovered that they were no longer there. He could move again.

His first thought was to go to the window, to see if they had somehow emerged into the street. Half of it was in sunlight, half in shadow. The vacancy of early afternoon held it in thrall. There was a tabby cat on a doorstep. A woman came out from one of the houses down the road; her face and gait were familiar to Kobus though he did not know her name. The wooden tray in which the baker's boy took around his wares every morning lay on the ground, with its heavy leather strap coiled on it.

17

This familiar scene was uncanny too: uncanny in its ordinariness, its ignorance of the encounter he had just been through.

Then Kobus said out aloud, 'What's the matter with you, you old fool? Why shouldn't your grandchildren come to play here? Their mother must have left them. Little Braam and . . . what's her name? . . . Thirza?'

But he heard in his own voice the falsity of what he was saying. Braam and Thirza, indeed! The children he had seen did not look like his recollection of Braam and Thirza. That he was certain of. Also that his grandchildren were older than these. And there was something else about them which was even stranger to him than their faces and figures.

Since when, he had to ask himself, did his grandchildren wear the clothes of the Christer — of the followers of Yeshua, Jesus, the Christus, the Natzerit, whatever they liked to call him? The one who had supposedly lived and died and lived again a thousand years before; or perhaps even more than that, for all bewildered Kobus could tell. The girl's cap; the boy's bare head; his red sleeveless jerkin: these were unmistakable signs. So were their little boots. For some reason, sunk beyond recall in an immemorial tradition or superstition, only they, the Christer, wore boots with buttons down the side; the God-Fearers never did. In his childhood Kobus and his friends had believed

18

devoutly that the Christers' boots had to be buttoned in that style because of some quality peculiar to pig-leather.

Even then it surprised him that he should have remembered such a thing so clearly – the buttons, that is, and the childish tale about them – when he recollected how long it was since he had last actually seen any of the Christer in the flesh. When the Amar Yotam had driven them away he had told the people that he was also driving away all their troubles. Famines, plagues, poverty, even their own stupidity.

The first sight of the children was inevitably etched with its own particular sharpness in Kobus's mind. But the other visits they made eventually ran together indistinguishably. Having come once, the children came before him again and again. Soon they had come so many times it was impossible for him even to estimate how often he had seen them. There were single days when he found himself sharing moments of their lives on perhaps half-a-dozen separate occasions. There were also days, and days following on days, when he saw them not at all, and began to assume or to hope that they had gone for good.

They never behaved in a manner that was at all out of the ordinary – apart, of course, from the inexplicability of their very presence, of their mode of manifesting themselves and then vanishing. The apparent ordinariness of their demeanour was itself one of the strangest things about them. It might have been (to judge from the way they looked and acted) that they had just returned from a walk, or had just eaten a meal, or were waiting for their mother to finish a task before taking them out of the house. The gestures of the girl's slender hands and the quiver of her lively brown eyes became familiar to Kobus; so did the boy's slouching or dragging walk, which had worn down the outer sides of the heels of his wooden-soled boots. More than that: as in some ineluctable dream, Kobus felt that everything about them had always been familiar to him; he had an intimacy with them which it was impossible for him to explain. In the presence of the children there was no need to explain it: he simply knew them, and had always known them, and that was all.

Yet this too was a source of fear and bewilderment. From where did this conviction come? Where had he met them before? How was it that he knew the slender column of the girl's upright, unlined neck, every pale curve and hollow of it; that he was sure he would recognise her voice if only she would speak to him; that her dresses and the stockings that went with them were to his eyes just as they should have been? And the red scratch that suddenly appeared on the back of the boy's hand – that too was known to him. The next time he came Kobus looked for it; and yes, it was still there; only it had darkened slightly, as it had begun to heal.

Yet of him, their watcher, their knower, their host, they took not the slightest notice. They looked at him and beyond him; they walked towards him and through him; he saw them in front of him and turned to find them behind him. Never a word did they say to him. Then they were gone. He saw them wear expressions angry, playful, absorbed, thoughtful; they talked to each other (inaudibly), smiled (at he knew not what), held hands, gazed out of his window, looked (as incomprehendingly as Elisabet herself) at the backs of the books on his shelves. Not a sound from them ever managed to reach his ears; and not a sound from his full breast and contracted throat and dry mouth apparently reached theirs.

So vivid they were, full-fleshed, space-occupying, light-blocking, at one instant; nothing at all the next. Each time they had gone, he remained staring at an emptiness which now contained not the faintest remembrance of their presence. No rug or pillow was disarranged, there was no scent in the air, nothing they might have touched was ever out of place.

A conversation.

Kobus: Elisabet, do you know if any of the Christer have come to live around here?

Elisabet: Ekh, pah, puh!

Kobus: Talk like a human being, for heaven's sake! Answer my question! Have you seen any Christer people wandering about town lately?

Elisabet (turning her head aside and miming the act of spitting): God forbid.

Kobus: No? None at all? No children running about?

Elisabet (with another mimed gob floorwards, and an indescribable puckering of her face, intended to combine disgust with religious fervour): He will preserve us.

Kobus: Would you know what they look like? How they dress?

Elisabet: Once when we went to Kraaifels, we saw some of the Christer — whole families of them. My cousins in Kraaifels told me that when they pass you in the street you have to look at them like this (sliding her eyes into their muddy corners and lowering her head) or they'll put a curse on you. Then you swell out here (pointing under her arms) and here (at her shrivelled groin) and afterwards you die.

Kobus: Really?

Elisabet: Master, everyone knows that.

Kobus: And everyone knows you're a stupid old woman.

Elisabet: Oh, master! Why stupid? It's not right to say such a thing to poor Elisabet. I try my best . . . (And so on.)

*

It had to be, Kobus decided, that his visitors were the products and he was the victim of a complex, recurring possession or hallucination of some kind.

From which there followed a question he had to put to himself, though he knew he would never be able to answer it. Which was worse, to have hallucinations without knowing you were doing so, or to have them and to be aware of what they were?

In a sense Kobus felt he had ample experience of both these states. Invariably he fell into the first when the childish apparitions were before him; then it was impossible for him not to accept wholeheartedly their reality. And he fell back into the second once they had gone; then he had to acknowledge them once again to have been nothing more in all likelihood than fantasies, figments of a diseased imagination.

His own, or some other person's? Was he really bewitched? Could it be that there was someone abroad who had procured these phantoms to appear before him? For a hard-headed man like Kobus, a scoffer at the superstitions of others, a despiser of Elisabet-like legends, it was a great humiliation even to harbour such suspicions.

Of one thing, though, he was certain. In neither state, whether the children were absent or present, was it possible for him to expel them through an exercise of will, or to prevent them from returning.

The efforts he had made to do so! The foolish ruses he had adopted! The unavailing runs he had made at them!

Yes, he did once actually run at them with his walking stick in his hand, shaking and whirling it like a madman, as if it would be able to strike against these airy creatures, and wound them, even leave their little corpses lying at his feet. But all it succeeded in doing, that stick of his, was to break a vase of glazed clay of which Rahella had been especially proud. (She claimed it had been brought to her father as a present from Aurinia.) Then see the madman sobbing as he picked up, with trembling fingers, the fragments of the vase . . . Or hear him speaking in gibberish at his apparitions, as if to conjure them away.

Or if it was not gibberish he uttered, then words he had never heard before and could not remember once they had been spoken.

Now listen to him, the madman, beseeching the children to show a little mercy to him. He is an old man, after all, they are young: why should they have come here to torment him? He is waiting to die, they have their whole lives in front of them . . .

Then the madman laughs at himself, not at them, and hits himself across the forehead.

What it would be like to have hallucinations which were inherently menacing and hideous –

monstrous animals and people, abysses, blood, God's eyes upon you – Kobus trembled to think. His hallucinations, the creatures who had come into his life, could not have been more juvenile, more harmless and domestic in appearance; nor more indifferent, it seemed, to his presence. Yet he knew how much they frightened him and how degraded they made him feel. Especially as he was convinced right from the start that if he let slip to others, even to Elisabet, the least word of what he was going through, his family would at once conclude that he was simply senile and crazy and would treat him as such. Hadn't he seen it happen to others, in his town and elsewhere, sometimes with people he had known well, even friends of his: old men and women, or crazy young ones, tied to posts, beaten with whips, starved so that the evil spirits inhabiting them might be starved too? Or simply put away in the country in the care of corrupt and vicious 'keepers'?

No thank you. And doubly no thank you once it occurred to him that no move of his, no change of his circumstances, would necessarily defeat the ghostly pertinacity of the children. True, he had seen them only in his own house, nowhere else – so far. But if he were to move to another house or another town, why should they not follow him? If they could walk through walls, vanish in an instant and instantly return, be seen by him and apparently never see him, why should so simple a trick as that of going to live with his daughter (say) or somewhere further afield cause them any discomfort or difficulty?

So all he could do was wait and hope that this 'phase', as he might have called it if only it were happening to someone else, would end as unexpectedly as it had begun. In the meantime he tried to get the upper hand of his visitors by fleeing, or by playing loudly at his rebeck, or by keeping his curtains closed all day in the hope that they would think the place was empty, or by praying for help to the God in whom he did not believe. (Needless to say, He quite properly failed to hear Kobus's pleas.) And since the children did not appear when Elisabet was in the house, he tried to think of ways of keeping her in the house instead of sending her away once her tasks were finished.

As he wandered about the town's streets and the lanes and fields beyond, an obvious and yet obviously mad question tormented him. Was his presence in the house necessary for the children to occupy it; or could they be there, at that very moment, while he was elsewhere?

Yes, he did return speedily sometimes, to try to catch them unawares; to catch them at it while they thought his back was turned.

But never with any success.

*

Many years before, in his youth, Kobus had once read a Yavanit legend about a man who was pursued by hideous, stinking creatures called the Eumenides, or the Furies. They were ghosts from his past, tormentors of his conscience. He constantly fled in terror from them and they as constantly followed him. Then there came a day when he stopped running, acknowledged to others their presence in his life, and confessed to the crime that had impelled the Furies to follow him. Once this confession was made, lo and behold, the creatures transformed themselves into his helpers, his understanders; their name was changed too, and they became the Friendly Ones. They actually helped him (if Kobus's recollection of the tale was correct) to start building a great new city, in which justice would reign.

Kobus would have hesitated on all sorts of grounds to compare himself with one of the ancient heroes of Yavan. And he would have hesitated even longer to compare his diminutive visitants with the terrifying, journeying creatures of the legend.

And yet . . .

What, he wondered, was the source of the power such stories had over us, if not in the chance they gave us to recognise ourselves in them, however feeble we might be, and however remote our lives might be in time and circumstances from the figures in the legends?

Yavan? Yavanit? Could that be right?

It hardly looked it. And what had been the hero's name? And his crime?

All he could remember was that he had been a prince of some kind.

Night now. Kobus stands at the window. The walls and roofs out there, touched fleetingly with star-light, hooded in shadow, tell him nothing; the moonless sky likewise. Every now and again a gust of wind comes and heaves clumsily at the branches of trees which rise above the roofs of the houses nearby; the wind bumps against the corner of the house, tries to get a grip on it, fails, goes off in a huff. (Precisely.) Kobus asks himself why someone as ordinary as himself should have the distinction of being haunted conferred on him. He had never been anyone of consequence. Even in the 'prime of life', what had he been? No prince, certainly. Just another man with a wife and a few children (one had died in infancy, poor thing, a little girl named Mariamme); and a printing and bookbinding shop, employing a few journeymen and an apprentice or two; and a house on the outskirts of town, with a long expanse of grass and some orchard-trees in front of it. What else had ever been special to him? A few unseemly, secret habits of an entirely trivial kind; and a friend or two; and an underlying sense of . . . futility, he supposed, or even of shame, at not having made more of himself.

In short, he had been like any other man of his

age and condition in that futile little town, with its view to the east of hills with raggedly wooded summits and their lower slopes neatly combed into vineyards, and flat plains (farms, grazing cattle, scrub) stretching to the big river in the west. If you went north along the muddy roads you would find other towns just like Niedering, with plenty of people just like Kobus in them, until you came to the biggest of them, Klaggasdorf. It was there, in Klaggasdorf, a long time before, that Kobus had served his apprenticeship under Hiram the Bookbinder.

How proud his father, Amos the Pedlar, had been when he had signed and paid in cash for his son's indentures, thus making sure that he would eventually occupy a higher social position than Amos himself ever had! Prince Kobus, indeed! And with what trepidation the boy had left home, just after his fourteenth birthday, to travel the hundred leagues to that unknown, mysterious destination!

Klaggasdorf . . . A name full of wonder and danger, it had seemed to Kobus then. The very sound of the syllables made his stomach flutter. Eleven years were to pass before he returned to Niedering, bringing with him his wife and his wife's dowry, to set up business on his own account. During those years he had left Klaggasdorf on just three or four occasions: when he came home to be with his father in his last illness; when he went with his master Hiram to the book-fair at Beeches; and during the time of the Ten Turmoils, for much the longest spell of all, when he fled into the countryside with Hiram's family to escape the dangers that had threatened them in town.

So much for the grand vicissitudes of his life. Who was he, a person with such a history, to be haunted by ghosts special to him? Let him assume that those little creatures were not hallucinations but really were messengers of some kind, nothing less than divine breaths or possibilities composed of some unthinkable substance, coming from some unknowable realm, having less understanding, perhaps, of their own mission or of who it was that gazed on them than a newborn baby does of its parents; assume also that they took human shape – even with Christer clothes on! – only so that they could be seen by him; and then let him go about the business of explaining to them who he was and what he was and the nature of his inconsequential circumstances . . . Making clear, as he did so, that these circumstances, for all their triviality, had always been more important in his life than his character. (Or could that in itself be a definition of his character?) Then let him go on to ask them humbly, in a language he had no reason to suppose they understood, what it was that they wanted of him.

A belated wish. Kobus wished that he had read less when he had been a young man. His life would probably have been happier for it, and his brain less confused in old age than it now was. There would have been less rubbish at loose in it, fewer jumbled notions of all kinds, and therefore less opportunity for confusion, for chaotic misplacings and misunderstandings.

It stood to reason.

Or if he was somehow bound to have been a reader, if it had been his fate to find the printed word irresistible, then let him at least have kept to the works assembled by the strictest of our commentators and moralists. Who knows, that too might have saved him from his present plight.

His wife — thinking of her he realised he had forgotten her name for the moment; but was confident it would come back to him sooner or later — his wife, whatever her name was, used to hate his reading. She was convinced that what he read was useless, speculative stuff, certain to prove a threat to his moral and spiritual safety. Also she hated the fact that reading gave him the chance to absent himself mentally from her and from the children.

Kobus had thought her a stupid woman, to tell the sad truth. (Since she had never been able to read what was in his mind, and was now as little able as Elisabet to read anything he might write down, why should he spare her feelings? Or his own?) As a young woman she had had fine grey eyes, and a slender figure, and hard, round, ruddy cheeks

which the newly-wed Kobus would lick and bite at
– quite fiercely, too, though never as fiercely as he
actually wanted to. He had not married her just for
her dowry; far from it. But he had soon learned
that her mind was narrow and conventional,
wholly preoccupied with what this woman had
said and that one had worn; what chickens cost
today and what cabbages might cost tomorrow.
Important questions, no doubt; but surely not the
only ones we had been put on earth to ask. The
result, anyhow, was that within a year or so of their
wedding he ceased to listen to her; over the half-
century and more that followed, he had hardly
heard a word she said. Not in any serious sense.

There must be many marriages like that. But
now – now – when it was too late to help either of
them, Kobus concluded that she had been right and
he had been wrong about the reading and the
habits of speculation on which he used to pride
himself.

Shit! That's what they were.

He had never been one for expletives. But there
was no other word to describe the random stuff
that seemed to be constantly swirling around in his
mind. He could actually feel it doing so, with a
slow, circular, unstoppable motion, like a vertigo.
Where did it all come from – these words unfamiliar to him even as he uttered them, these histories
he did not understand, these speculations of which
he felt himself to be the victim rather than the

master – if not from the useless books he had devoured with such hunger so long ago? And was that not also the truth about the little ghosts who appeared and disappeared before him, inside his own house, just as they pleased?

Not content with tormenting him in his waking hours, it seemed, they now sent strange dreams to him at night; dreams in which he knew them to be participants, though they never showed themselves to his dreaming eye. *That* they saved for his waking gaze.

You were right, Rahella! he wanted to exclaim to her. (There, her name had come back to him, as he had been sure it would.) Instead of sitting at home reading his books he would have done far better to spend evening after evening in the nearest tavern, exchanging inanities and profanities with whatever idiots had happened to be there. Rahella wouldn't have liked that either; but perhaps he would have been more at peace with himself than he now was.

In his dream, later that night, Kobus found himself in the middle of a muddy, treeless plain which stretched away as far as he could see in every direction. Incongruously dotted at random about it were a great number of bare, wooden, kitchen tables. Night had fallen. The only light came from flickering lanterns which had been placed on the tables. Seated at each one of them was a man who appeared to be busy writing down names on a scroll or studying names that were already on it. All around them were hundreds, even thousands, of people. They were ceaselessly on the move, hurrying from table to table, pushing and shoving at each other, looking around, gathering in anxious clusters, crying out and gesturing imploringly at the seated clerks, breaking away to go to the next table, the next point of light, and the one beyond, and the one beyond that.

Everything was out in the open, with not a roof, not a fence, not so much as a plank of wood anywhere to serve for shelter. And with no end to any of it.

Christer, these desperate people were, all of them. Kobus knew it. He knew also that they had been told they must find their names and their children's names on one or another of the scrolls the officials were handling. They imagined that if they did as they had been told to do, if they found the right table, the right clerk, the scroll with their names on it, they would be recognised, redeemed, sent to some place of safety. But Kobus knew better. It was all a charade. The officials were not really reading the scrolls in front of them, they were writing down none of the names the people were calling out so urgently to them. Nothing the people did would make the slightest difference to their fate. None whatever. There was no release, no hope, for any of them.

Somewhere among them also, Kobus knew, 'his'

two children were to be found in that great field. Or were not to be found. Their case was no different from that of all the others.

That's how it was in his dream. The men at the tables were God-Fearers too, just like Kobus. So much like him, indeed, that from one moment to the next, without his being aware of how it had happened, he had ceased to be an onlooker, a bewildered visitor to this place of mud and misery, and had become one of the officials, with a table and a lamp and a scroll of his own to take charge of. There it was in front of him, the scroll, just like the paper on which he spent some of his time, these days, writing at his desk. In fact, what he was doing in the dream was somehow indistinguishable from what he did at his desk; the two activities were mysteriously one. Yet seated at this table, he wrote nothing down, for he had nothing to write with; and he read nothing too, for the inscriptions on the scroll were illegible, markings merely, packed indecipherably together. Yavanit those marks could have been, for all he could understand of them; or like those incomprehensible strips and blocks of picture-writing which the Mitzrim used to carve on their great tombs and statues. When Kobus looked up he saw a multitude of faces within the space which the lamp on his table shiveringly illumined: faces of strangers, scores of them, always changing. Distorted with fear and beseeching, all were turned to him. Clean-shaven men, women in white embroidered caps, young and old, looking at him as if he could help or save them if he wished, or at the very least tell them what they should do next and what was going to happen to them. But he knew nothing, except that he had found himself in the midst not only of misery, but of terror: terror now and greater terror still to come.

The legs of the chair he was sitting on sank a little further into the mud; and he thought to himself, prosaically enough, and yet with panic in his breast, as if this were the source of their fear and his own (and yet knowing it was not; that what was hidden from him was worse by far): How will we manage if it rains? Have the people in charge thought about *that*? And even as the question passed through his mind he felt the first small drops on his face; innocent drops, only a few of them, meaning no harm, falling for no other reason than that the conditions – the circumstances! – were right for them to do so; and yet capable of drenching everyone there, chilling them, making them suffer.

He would be all right, he would find a dry place eventually; of that Kobus was convinced. He held an official position, he had a piece of paper curled up importantly in front of him, to confirm the status he held. But them? The wretched Christer, these obstinate Jesus-people in their thousands, stretching away across the plain? Obedient to their orders, or to what they took to be their orders, they

36

ran past and jostled one another, tripped, fell, cried out, looking for the one spot in that endless, sordid plain which they imagined would mean safety to them; and which he knew they would never find. There were babes in arms, mothers holding their children by the hand, children lost and crying for their mothers, old people who stared about them or had simply given up, and squatted or lay in the mud.

Nothing else 'happened' in his dream – other than the horror he felt at the place, and at his being there; and the struggle he went through in order to get away from it, which he knew he could do only by waking. That he struggled to release himself, struggled towards wakefulness, he knew; he was aware of it while the dream still continued; but what form the struggle took was hidden from him.

It was an unspeakable relief to wake up. There he was in his bed, nowhere else, Kobus the printer, the ex-printer, the former bookbinder; no one else; nowhere else. The lamp he had left burning when he had fallen asleep was still alight; but the window was now filled with a dark blue, almost purple light. Dawn would soon follow. He had nothing to fear or to be ashamed of.

Then, remotely and yet with a feeling of dismayed recognition quite unlike the dread he had experienced during his dream, yet worse than that experience because he was now awake, and knew it, he remembered a sight he had witnessed during

37

the time of the Turmoils. This was no dream at all; but a recollection returning after decades of absence. He had been on his own, on foot, somewhere in the country, following a lane that ran between two rough hedgerows. He heard an unlikely sound in that isolated setting; then, through a gap in the hedge, he found himself looking on a field that was full of Christer people. This field was quite unlike the one in his dream. It was small, not a huge plain. It was surrounded by scrubby, hedgelike growth. No tables were to be seen there and no officials; it was daylight, not evening; dry, not wet. The people in the field were also unlike those in the dream: they were motionless, exhausted, all but silent, sitting or lying wherever they had fallen on the grass. The only noise was that of the crying of a few children. That was the unexpected sound he had heard.

Kobus had no idea how long the people had been there, where they had come from, where they were going. But he did know enough not to ask such questions of them or of anyone else he might meet. He hurried past.

Still, the fact was that he had never felt any hostility to the Christer, even in the so-called good or bad old days, when it was possible to see them almost everywhere. He had never regarded them as threatening or disgusting. He did not believe the stories some people loved to tell about them: about the diseases they were supposed to carry; about the cannibal feasts they went in for; about the plans they had to take over (with the help of the evil spirits they had at their command) the governance of the world; and all the rest of the rubbish one heard in those days. And not only in those days, as Elisabet had just made plain to him. Even in the time of the persecutions, even when his ex-friend Malachi had gone around the country preaching against them, and preaching no less fiercely to those who were not enthusiastic enough in waging war against them, even then Kobus's motto had been: Live and let live. It wasn't in his nature to think ill of people simply because their customs differed from his own or because they held beliefs he did not share. After all, if belief was in question – how many people right there in Niedering, his home town, shared his own *lack* of belief?

So what was it that was wanted of him now? Why did Christer spectres haunt him: innocent children by day, and distraught throngs of them, whole populations, by night?

Some days or weeks went by; Kobus could not have said how many of either. The only certainty about this period, the only term which he could put to it, was that it had led up to his suffering yet another heavy fall. Another 'accident'.

This one happened just after he had returned from what he had deemed to be a successful trip to the earth-closet outside the house. (Success in that operation was not always to be taken for granted.) It was morning; he was downstairs; alone. He put his foot on the first step and without warning the whole house seemed to rear up behind him. It was black, and of a great height and weight; it came over his head like a huge cowl of timber and mortar, and it roared deafeningly as it came, blotting out everything but itself.

He had a space in his consciousness for just one thought before he was overwhelmed: Is this how it comes? – 'it' being of course the end of everything; his end.

Some time later he became aware that his eyes were open. He was looking upwards. The two children were looking down at him. Nothing could have been more remote from the roaring blackness which had felled him than the delicacy and concern of their expression. It was clear that they were anxious not only for him but for themselves too; they looked at him with the dismay that children of flesh and blood might have shown, had they come to visit him from next door and found him lying there.

He felt an almost languid pleasure in his helplessness before them; and in the guiltlessness of it, too, since the alarm he was causing was not of his wish, and hence hardly of his doing. But within the pleasure lurked a disappointment too. So it had not been the end of everything, after all. That would still have to be gone through: all of it; as far as consciousness could take him; and then beyond.

It was just at that moment, looking up, marvelling doubtfully at his still being there to look at them, that he knew a great change had taken place. The identity of the children was no longer a secret to him.

He had no sense of having made a discovery; rather it was like having found, moments before, that his eyes were already open, even though he had no recollection of opening them. Nothing could have been simpler; nothing more self-evident.

Hours later, or a moment later – impossible again for him to tell which – a face of a very different kind hung over him. It was wrinkled, female, brownish; he recognised it immediately but could not give it a name. He wanted to tell this person about the children having been there earlier, and how he had recognised them. But the task was beyond him. Perhaps, he thought, if he moved his hand just *so* his meaning would be clear.

That much of a gesture he did manage to make, but to what effect he could not say.

Then the face of another female appeared. The name attached to this one he knew at once, and said it, or thought he said it.

The woman's lips moved, they quivered into life; her eyes filled with tears.

'Father,' he heard her say.

So she was his daughter . . . While he mused over the unexpectedness of this claim, and also over the fact that he was no longer lying on the floor, but could feel bedclothes above and beneath him, she went away and the darkness returned.

Subsequently he found himself at his desk, more or less dressed, more or less in command of himself. It seemed remarkably soon for him to have managed to get there, considering the violence of the fall he had suffered. But how soon it actually had been he did not know. All he was certain of was that yet another encounter – a conversation, indeed – with his daughter had taken place in between.

They had talked about the children. He told her he had seen them earlier, and asked her where they were now. She answered readily enough, 'Oh, they're at home.'

'At home? You know where they live?'

She looked at him askance. 'Of course I do. They're at home with Shem.'

'Shem?'

'Yes, he's looking after them while I'm away.'

'Is he their father?'

Another sharp, doubtful look came his way. 'Of course he is. You know that.'

'They're very nice, the children,' he said. 'What are their names?'

'Braam and Thirza and Franke.'

'Three of them?'

'Of course.'

'It's funny that I never see the three of them together. Only two of them, always, the boy and the girl. Just the two of them.'

'Father! What are you saying? You've often seen all of them together.'

'No, just the two. And always they're dressed so strangely, like little Christer.'

'Dressed like little Christer? My children? That's . . .' She paused, and caught her breath, and chose a softer word than the one which had evidently been rising to her lips. 'That's silly.'

It was obvious to him that she was telling the truth, or what she believed to be the truth. She went on chidingly. 'Braam, Thirza and Franke are your grandchildren. I'm their mother. You know that . . . I think you should rest now, Father. You're a little confused, I can see it. You'll feel better when you've had a sleep.'

'Perhaps I will.'

His docility seemed to surprise her. In fact he wanted her out of the room, so that he could think over what she had said. She was his daughter: that claim he did believe, even though he could not reconcile this mature, worn woman, whose tired brow and anxious eyes regarded him so keenly, with the little girl who had really been his daughter. That one, the daughter he remembered, had had thin upper arms and plump, pale cheeks, and was always ready to hold his hand when they walked

43

together in the street. How could this woman and that little girl possibly be the same person?

Besides, the children she was talking about were clearly not the ones who had taken to visiting him.

So he closed his eyes and pretended to sleep, just as she had told him to, as if he were an obedient child and she his mother. In the darkness he heard the rustle of her clothes about the room while she performed a few tasks. It was a familiar, soothing sound, which reminded him of his wife. He could not think for the moment where she might be, that wife of his. Then the door closed and he was on his own. Presently he heard the street door close. At once he got out of bed and came downstairs with the vague idea of going to his desk.

It was on his way down that he became conscious of a new trouble which had overtaken him. His left arm and leg seemed to have become more distant from him than they used to be; they were certainly more sluggish than they should have been. Whenever he made a demand of them they obeyed him only after a perceptible pause. It did not matter what the demand was. Walk, stretch, turn over a page, lift a finger: always he had to wait for the act to take place. Almost as surprising as this strange, localised recalcitrance was the reminder it gave him of the obedience from all the different parts of himself which he had hitherto been able to take for granted.

Fortunately for him, it was his right hand, not his

left, which had always been his favourite slave. At least that one still did its work unquestioningly.

He was not to remain in solitude for long. While he was still seated at his desk a whole deputation came to visit him. There was his daughter, her husband Shem, their three children, and also, as a bonus, Shem's elderly mother. After a short interval they were joined by his son, to whom a message had evidently been sent. They all expressed concern at finding him out of his bed, and tried to hurry him back into it. But he resisted their demands: partly out of obstinacy, but also because he had not had time to hide his papers before the visitors had come in. He was afraid the scraps he had just written would be found once he was out of the room and in his bed. And then? Who knew what conclusions they would draw from them; or, even worse, what they would do once they had drawn their conclusions? Sitting at the desk, his papers partially covered with books and with his shawl, which he had clumsily thrown across the desk as soon as he had heard the front door open, he looked from face to face among those confronting him – child's face, adult's face, crone's face – all apparently so anxious on his behalf. As he did so he found to his astonishment that what he actually wanted was to confide in them.

Such a relief it would be no longer to hide anything from them: neither the visits the children had made to him, nor his certainty that he now knew exactly who they were.

But it could not be done. None of them would understand. They would not believe a word he said to them. He could see it in their faces. It was the very quality of their concern that made it plain to him. They felt sorry for him. They found him absurd and pathetic. They would never believe his story. Or they would believe that he believed it; but that would be all the more reason for them to dismiss it. What would he himself think, if he could see himself sitting there, half-dressed, a dishevelled old man hugging a dishevelled desk?

In the end he came to a compromise with them and himself. He did tell them the truth – in a sense. Of the children, his secret children, he was careful to say nothing directly. But of his daughter's children, his grandchildren, he did speak. Naming them one by one (Braam, Thirza, and . . . oh yes, Franke), he told them that one day, soon, he would be gone, and everything that had happened to him, all the memories of which he was the sole guardian, would vanish for ever. None of them, let alone the children they would have when they were adults, would have any conception of his life, or of the life that their great-grandfather, Amos the Pedlar, had led, or of what their grandmother had been like as a young woman, and how he had met and married her. That was why he had started making some notes about his life which he would show them before too long. Think how lucky he was in having grandchildren who might read such notes, and how lucky they were in having a grandfather who wished to reach beyond them to the children they might one day have. Think of childless men and women; of parentless children; of children who perhaps waited in another world for a chance of life which would never be given to them . . .

And so on. There was enough truth in what he was saying, or it was close enough to his present preoccupations, to move him as he spoke, and therefore to affect them as well. The result was that they solemnly withdrew from the room while he concealed the papers in the best place he could think of, which was behind a low oaken chest against the wall. Then he opened the door and told them he was now ready to return to his bed. In their eyes there was that special, kindly, humouring glint with which old people are invariably obliged to become familiar. As many as twenty-five years, perhaps, had passed since he had first been the victim or beneficiary of it; but never before had he seen it shine as strongly out of so many faces at one moment as it did then.

No matter.

Then the children came again. He thought they really were going to speak to him this time, so alive and full of understanding was their expression. The girl's slight chest heaved. He saw it do so, though he could not take his eyes from hers.

Now. Now.

But she did not speak.

He said, as gently as he could, 'I know who you are. I know who sent you here.'

Again he waited. It seemed to him that she was waiting too. Her eyes still held his. She was the elder of the two, the more aware; also, he was sure, the stronger. The eyes he was looking into were especially familiar to him: their shape as well as their keen brown colour, and the black line her eyebrows made above them, so clearly defined, so different in texture from the tender skin out of which they sprang. On either side of her nose these brows curved in steeply, in almost hook-like fashion; yet so delicately.

He knew them. Just such eyes had looked into his before, under the same intent, delicate brows. And from no further away than they were from him now.

'You look just like Sannie,' he said. 'I saw it this morning. Was it this morning? When the house fell on me, then I remembered.'

Still no answer. It was an effort for him to release his gaze from hers. But he would have done wrong to neglect the boy; perhaps, it occurred to him, the boy was in greater need of encouragement than the girl. He met the old man's gaze sturdily enough, as a freckled, self-conscious fellow should. Then

Kobus found words to distinguish between the children; he did not utter them but they seemed not at all absurd to him; so infatuated was he with their phantom lives: Her soul is deeper than his.

'When I was lying on the ground,' he said aloud, 'it came to me. I opened my eyes and there you were. Suddenly I knew it.'

He held out his hands to them, one hand to each. But it was to the girl he spoke.

'You look just like little Sannie in Klaggasdorf. Just as she used to look. You could be her, I promise you. Except you're even younger than she was in those days, when I knew her. Are you her daughter? Her granddaughter? Her great-granddaughter? Is that why you've come to me?'

She had listened intently; now she opened her mouth. At last she was about to speak to him. He leaned forward, anxious not to miss a word she said.

Inches from his face was a closed door. He was staring at it. Or it was staring at him. He knew every dint and crack and stain in its broad planks. Now the bolt yielded to his tugging with its usual groan.

Once the door was open he stared up and down the empty street. Nobody was about. The light of day was everywhere: that shadowless light which a summer's day enjoys long before the sun has risen. He was in his night-clothes. His feet were bare. He

49

must have got out of bed and come downstairs, though he could remember nothing of it.

The smell of baking, like a sweet, corrupting taint, suddenly came to him from the bakery across the street. The air had been free of it just a moment before.

He called out into the emptiness, 'Sannie! Sannie!'

The noise was so loud, to his ears, he was sure it would be heard in all the houses around. But no one stirred.

And again. 'Sannie!'

That was how, nearly seven decades before, the widow from the house alongside had always called her. Always with the same lengthening of the last syllable. 'San*nie*! San*nie*!'

Then one would hear her rapid, clacking footsteps, and a subdued, 'Yes M'sies.'

But this time: nothing.

TWO

Only during his apprenticeship in Klaggasdorf had Kobus ever really come into close contact with any of the Christer people. In those days there was quite a big community of them in the town. They must have made up almost a fifth of its population. The Christer had been something of a rarity at home in Niedering; they would appear only sporadically and then go off again, following the peripatetic trades special to them. The community in Klaggasdorf was quite different, not just because of its size but also because of its settled nature. To Kobus, the newly arrived apprentice, the presence of these alien people was just one aspect of the general strangeness, even the exoticism, of the place.

Klaggasdorf lay only about a hundred leagues from Niedering, but to his juvenile eye the differences between the two towns were overwhelming. First, Klaggasdorf was much bigger than his home town. From that difference all the others seemed to flow. Its market square and public buildings were more imposing than any he had seen before. There were walls around the town; ruinous in parts, well-preserved in others. The houses in Klaggasdorf were built not of plaster and lath as those in Niedering were, but of a greyish brick of river clay, and roofed with orange and yellow tiles. From a distance the roofs looked as if they were all joined together; they made up a terrain across which (Kobus's daydreams told him) a man might wander for days, if only he could get up there.

Alongside the town ran a real river, not a stream like the one on which Niedering stood, and there was another town, Postmasfurt, on the far bank, with a ferry boat (and a hawser, and a horizontal wooden wheel, and the power of four donkeys, and the shouts and whip of the donkey-driver) to join the two. At the town's quay river-barges offloaded grain and seacoal, and took on timber and bales of wool. The constant traffic had polished the broad wooden beams on the upper side of the quay, and they shone almost as brightly as the river itself when the sun stood directly overhead, or when it set somewhere behind ever-silent, distant Postmasfurt. But underneath, where the water lapped, those same timbers were roughened, softened, lightless, smelling of rot.

How clearly it all returned to Kobus; never more clearly than in what he believed (intermittently) to be his eighty-fourth year! How full of light and colour it was! It tempted him to imagine what he knew to be untrue: that the past, and the past alone, was forever without ambiguity.

Another difference: the main roads and the market square in Klaggasdorf were paved with stone slabs, not cobbles. To the east of the town, away from the river, were two high wooded hills, one of them with the ruins of a fort on it, to which Hiram the Bookbinder sometimes led his apprentices on their Sabbath outings. From there one could look westwards to the river, and eastwards to the serrated slopes of forest that rose to the horizon, with innumerable incisions of dim light and subtle shadow between the slopes. It was impossible for Kobus not to think of those dark mountainous masses as another dream-like terrain which one could walk on, clamber over, vanish into.

Oh, to him Klaggasdorf was exotic all right; and perhaps the most exotic thing about it, ultimately, was that to the people who had grown up there it was not exotic at all. To them *he* was the stranger; and everything about their town was perfectly ordinary, wholly to be taken for granted. Again and again he would try to imagine himself as someone who had grown up in Klaggasdorf, and in that role he would attempt to think of Niedering (of all improbable places) as exotic . . . and fail, of course. Yet the natives of Klaggasdorf were bound to wonder, as he did, at the differentness of places and people other than their own, Niedering included; and the same would be true wherever he went, and whoever he spoke to, even in the most distant corners of the world.

But then, the very idea of some corner of the world being 'distant' to those who actually lived there was in itself absurd; to them it would always be familiar, banal, unmysterious.

Exoticism, it seemed, was always in the eye of the beholder: a bewildering and disappointing thought, Kobus found it. Or was it ordinariness that really lay in the beholder's eye? If he had been born elsewhere, or at another time, or under some other order, he would have believed those circumstances commonplace, whatever they were; and the life he now led would have had all the allure of difference, even of topsy-turvydom.

Inversions of any kind, it seemed, were always thinkable by us, at least, even if never truly available to us.

Kobus did not speak of his broodings on this subject to anyone, not even to his best friend in Klaggasdorf, a student by the name of Malachi. He feared that he would be laughed at if he did, or that others (Malachi included) would simply fail to see what he was talking about. Later he was to dismiss these reflections as the fruit of nothing more than adolescence and home-sickness – both of which go on for ever, apparently, until they come to an end.

So, boylike, he more or less forgot all about it.

Niedering receded from his mind. The life he was leading drove out the thought of the life he had led previously, and of the other lives he might have led.

His days he spent in Hiram's workshop, learning the elements of his trade: its smells, sounds, textures, and drills of eye and hand. Eventually, he began to learn some of its satisfactions too. At night he slept in the big room under the tiled roof, along with three other apprentices and one journeyman. In the room next door slept the female servants of the household. Below were Hiram and his family. A small, wispily bearded man with a bony nose and intensely blue eyes set remarkably close on either side of it, he was a fierce but kindly employer. Kobus was always frightened by the discrepancy between the customary vagueness of Hiram's manner and the sharpness of his gaze when he examined his own work or that of others. His two eyes then seemed to his awed apprentice to become like one. It was from the respect he felt for Hiram and for his work that Kobus learned eventually to respect his own.

Their hours were long and Hiram's wife did not believe in spoiling the boys; they ate bread and gruel and cabbage, with meat or fish only on the Sabbath eve. The money they were given (very little of it) they spent mostly on items of food bought on the market square. The house was hot in summer, stiflingly so, especially in the attic – those nights unforgotten by him: unable to sleep, longing to

55

sleep, gasping for air! – and cold in winter. Every winter he got chilblains on his fingers, toes, and the tips of his ears; these would eventually open and turn into sores which nothing but the coming of summer would cure.

In short, his life was like that of every reasonably well-treated apprentice. Upstairs in the attic the boys (and the journeyman) sometimes indulged in certain games with each other of which they never dared speak in daylight hours to one another. By contrast, the grabs and shoves they made at the women servants next door were the occasion for loud boastings. They eyed the Tzigani and Christer girls whom they passed in the street, and made it their business to keep an eye (pretending they were not doing so, of course) on the town's two discreet houses of ill-repute, which they were neither brave nor wealthy enough to enter. One of those houses had the distinction of keeping a Kushi woman, said to be from Habbash, in the remote south; hoping for they knew not what, marvelling at the duskiness of her skin and trying to imagine that hue all over, the boys used to follow her when she walked down the street. They swam in the river when they could and tried to catch fish in it. They chased Christer urchins down lanes and alongside the city walls whenever they outnumbered them sufficiently, and shouted the traditional terms of abuse at them. Pig-eaters. Blood-drinkers. Yeshuaites. Cross-bones. Cross-breeds. Cross-pieces. And so forth. As well as that oath which, in the mouths of those who cried it out and in the minds of those at whom it was cried, was both the most obscure and the most insulting of all: *grave-robbers.*

As he grew taller and thinner, a miserable moustache began to sprout on Kobus's upper lip, then an even more miserable beard manifested itself, as well as the usual gross tufts of hair elsewhere. On holy days Hiram's men and boys dressed up and filed into the House of Prayer behind their master; so did all the other apprentices in town behind theirs. (In Niedering there had been just two places of worship; here there were several, including one belonging to the small but widely dispersed sect of the Noble Vine, who stubbornly claimed that they and they alone were the true descendants of Israel, the sole heirs of the promise made to the Yehudim of ancient times.) Anything the least bit out of the ordinary became the subject of prolonged discussion among household servants, journeymen, and apprentices. They were experts on the illness, death, pregnancy, elopement, drunkenness, and marital feuding of people they knew and people they did not know. Events like public executions (stoning) and public punishments (whipping), fires, mad dogs, rumours of buried treasure, the arrival of a boat, even the appearance of an outsize turnip in the marketplace, could keep them going for a day or days, even weeks. As a source of entertainment and education, gossip meant far more to them than the prayers they offered, the work they did, the games they tried to play, the music they made. Gossip was the line that attached them to one another and to the world beyond. Like donkeys tied to a wheel, they were forever winding it in, winding it out, to the sound of their own coughs and brays.

It was quite a common thing in those days for the wealthier families in Klaggasdorf to employ Christer servants. (Hiram did not.) This was especially true of their women, who worked as nursemaids, cooks, washerwomen, attendants to the sick, and so forth. Some of the menfolk, too, were employed domestically. They were often used for carrying out tasks on the Sabbath which were forbidden to their employers. But on the whole even those Christer men who were happy to see their wives and daughters in service preferred to stick to the trades traditional to them: masonry, wood and metal working, transport-riding, brewing, glazing, and several others. Some worked the land too. Many acquired a fair degree of wealth, all things considered, though they generally lived modestly enough. For the most part they lived to the north of the town, beyond the walls, in a few long streets that ran parallel to the river.

Kobus and his friends did not often wander down those streets, not because they were afraid to do so, but simply because there was nothing in particular they needed that could be found there. Only the lure of difference! For them that difference was most significantly embodied in the two churches the Christer maintained down there: both of them plain, rectangular buildings adorned with tapering towers and the cruciform symbol of the faith celebrated within. A mystic and yet threatening sign, the footloose, curious youngsters thought it. Along with his friends Kobus used to listen to the incomprehensible chanting, bell-ringing and sudden silences that came from the buildings when services were taking place; sometimes, without success, they tried to peer inside to see what was going on. Once or twice their giggles and scuffles with one another led to members of the congregation emerging to give them chase; then they fled, more in mirth than alarm, to the safety of the main streets of the town.

Each of the two churches down there, they knew, represented a separate branch of the faith the Christer held; they knew too that there were deep doctrinal disputes between the factions, which had led to much bitterness and bloodshed in the past, and would no doubt do the same again, if conditions permitted. The nature of the disputes that divided them was occasionally a subject for confident and ill-informed debate among the majority. It had something to do with how the Christer conceived the theophagous ritual at the heart of their worship – that much was certain. But what, exactly? In conversation with one another Kobus and his friends would solemnly put forward their opinions on the subject.

Exoticism at work again! The nakedness of the shaven faces of their menfolk was a constant reminder of how different they were from the majority; and so were the shamelessly uncut prepuces concealed within every pair of Christer breeches. One of the prizes of a successful pursuit of a Christer urchin was that you and your chums then had the opportunity to pull down his lower garment and to gaze your full, with fascination and disbelief, at the strangely elongated, faceless, wormlike object thus revealed.

All right. No messing about. No excuses. Consider how sinister the Christer were bound to appear to the more stupid and suspicious inhabitants of a place like Niedering. Or a place like Klaggasdorf. Or ten thousand smaller and larger places like them.

Now: did Kobus really suppose himself, then or later, to have been immune to what was said and thought by most of the people around him?

Of course he was not. Nobody was.

Take the eating habits of the Christer, merely, and think of the terms in which they were generally spoken of. Even Kobus's mild and good-humoured father, Amos the Pedlar, a man who would never hurt a fly, as people said – even he was a case in point. Here was a little group of people, Kobus remembered Amos telling him on more than one occasion, who were permitted by their religion (alone among the religions of the world, he would insist) to eat absolutely *anything*; and what was more, to eat their anythings and everythings in whatever promiscuous order and fashion they fancied: cooked, raw, in their shells and outside them, boiled in their own blood or milk, in any kind of vessel and from any kind of plate. All that on the one hand – and here Amos the Pedlar would drop his voice in dismay, coupled with a kind of amused incredulity – and on the other hand these same omnivores actually made the eating of their God's flesh and the drinking of his blood the culminating moment in their act of worship! This consumed and reborn God, remember, being the one whom they claimed to be the true God, our God, the God who had initially revealed himself to the Yehudim of ancient times, but utterly transformed from what He had been then. This deity of the Christers was humanised, though still divine; divided and yet mystically reunited with himself: tortured but all-powerful; ineffable but nevertheless pictured over and over again in their places of worship, along with his broodingly tender young mother, as infant, child, man in torment, God in majesty.

Our God, indeed! The impudence of it! Inevitably, there were many people among the God-Fearers who felt irked, offended in a curiously personal fashion, even enraged by the claims the Christer made: above all, by their claim that they alone were the elect, the chosen ones, the inalienable heirs of the promise. Especially as everything about their puny numbers compared with ours, their abject state contrasted with ours, proclaimed to anyone with eyes in his head how much we were in the right and they forever in the wrong. Pathetically in the wrong (if you wanted to be charitable in thinking about them); madly or blasphemously wrong (if you were of a less forgiving disposition).

Still, no one talked then, so far as Kobus could recall, of wiping them out or of expelling them to distant lands. That was to come later. They may have been disliked and slighted by many, even feared superstitiously by those who accused them of fanciful crimes and even more fanciful schemes for the future. But murder, therefore? Wholesale expulsion, despoliation? No one dreamt of it; not seriously, anyway. Because they had always been there, in greater or lesser numbers, it was more or less assumed they would always continue to be there. In any case, the God-Fearers were so divided among themselves, there were so many opposing tendencies and races and fiefdoms among them, who were so busy arguing and at times warring over inextricably intermingled issues of faith and language and sovereignty, territorial entitlement and extra-territorial privilege, that the doings of a marginal group like the Christer could ultimately appear inconsequential to them, neither here nor there. From east to west, from rainy Anglia to savage Russ, the God-Fearers and all their leaders had more important matters to think about: Saddukim (so-called) versus Perushim (so-called); both parties versus priestly, apocalyptic and messianic groupings of various kinds; royal or would-be-royal representatives of the Davidic line (so-called) versus the Hasmonai (self-styled), as well as those who claimed legitimacy from this or that Romait emperor; not to speak of the multitude of other factions and divisions which sometimes coincided with and more often cut across all these . . .

No, they had quite enough to keep even the more speculative of them busy with preoccupations of their own. And, as always, most of the people, most of the time, had their pressing, private affairs to think about: deaths, feasts, illnesses, the depredations of the taxmen their rulers constantly sent among them.

Ancient history. Where did they all go, the people Kobus used to see around him in Klaggasdorf, God-Fearers and Christer alike? He might as well have asked what happens to yesterday's clouds, or where the wind goes after it has ceased to blow.

Sitting in Niedering, nearly three-quarters of a century after his apprenticeship had ended, waiting for the return of the only Christer who ever appeared before him now, those ghostly children, his little Furies, Kobus asked himself a question of a different kind, or rather a whole series of questions, to which he could give no answer. But that did not make them any the less urgent to him. On the contrary.

What would have happened, he wondered, if history had taken a different turn when Roma had ruled what it chose to regard as the entire civilised world? What if the Yehudim of those times had *not* persisted, or had not been allowed to persist, with the great task they had then begun, and which the very existence of the imperial order made conceivable and, so, possible: namely, that of winning over to the worship of the one true God whatever pagan peoples they found themselves among; the Romaim most definitely included? What if those who had responded to that call, the very first to give themselves the name of the God-Fearers, had for some reason come to be seen by the imperial authorities as traitors, outlaws, enemies of the empire? (After a rebellion in the Holy Land, say?) What then? Imagine the might of the empire, with all its disciplined savagery, turned irrevocably against them. What would have been their circumstances, his circumstances, our circumstances, then?

And by 'then' he meant: now, that day, that night.

A mad fantasy? No doubt. Even to an inveterate sceptic like Kobus it had the look of a kind of blasphemy. Another history! Another past for half the human race!

Yet it could have happened that way. That was more or less how it had happened to those wretched Christer, after all.

Hadn't it?

Another imagining.

Kobus tried to imagine how it would have been if the Christer had seized on the opportunity he had just retrospectively given them; if they had been able to emerge from their caves and corners to carry abroad the message of their Saviour's death and resurrection. Imagine that in so doing they had successfully directed against their rivals all the malign accusations the Romaim had made against themselves: from the drinking of blood to the devouring of children, from the worship of asses to an incessant scheming to seize power worldwide. And had added to these charges that of deicide, the killing of their God, of everyone's God, too!

What, Kobus wondered, would that have made of himself? Of Elisabet? Neighbours all? And of his neighbours in Klaggasdorf some seventy years years before: the widow and her children; Malachi who boarded in their house; and their Christer servant Sannie?

This Sannie had been the only servant in the household next door to Hiram's. (Except, Kobus corrected himself, for an older woman who came in once a week to take the washing down to the river, where she would languidly beat the garments with stones, like condemned felons, before hanging them out on bushes to dry.) Sannie, helped by the daughters of the household, and urged on by the widow's scoldings, did the rest. She washed the dishes, made the beds, tended the pots hanging on hooks above the hearth, swept the floors, carried the slops to the midden, sewed, scraped mud off boots. She was about the same age as the widow's youngest daughter: fourteen, at most. The line of her developing bust was hardly more prominent than that of the long rib-cage which supported it. She had a long neck and waist, too, which suggested how tall she would be when she was fully grown. On her head she wore the cap appropriate to an unmarried Christer female; on her feet clumsy wooden clogs (a mark of her poverty, not of her religion) and coarse, wrinkled stockings of some woollen material.

Kobus, alone in his house in Niedering, waiting still for the return of his ghosts, now remembered it all so clearly. The look of the house from the outside; the widow's grown and semi-grown children, whose names he was suddenly almost sure of (Essep? Saul? Dora?); and the sound of their voices; the big room with the hearth across one wall, where the family ate and had its rows and where Sannie slept overnight, on a straw pallet, under the big table. They were a noisy lot, the widow and her children. Even when they were on good terms with one another their voices were raised like those of people having an argument; when they quarrelled, which they often did, they shouted and wept, abused one another and banged plates and slammed doors. These outbursts were followed by almost equally rowdy reconciliations. (Hiram's house, by contrast, was a quiet, orderly place; it was his nature, and that of his wife, to keep it so; even the printshop was invariably in a neater condition than any Kobus was to see later, his own included.)

There were two centres of silence in that household: Malachi was one, Sannie the other. It was for the sake of the first that Kobus visited the house. Of the second, little Sannie, he scarcely took notice. She was merely the Christer skivvy; one more like others to be found in households all over Klaggasdorf. Some of them pattered home to their quarter – the Mishkennet, it was called – at the end of each day; others, like Sannie, only after the end of the Sabbath, so that she might spend the next day, her day of rest and worship, with her family. Where exactly she lived in the Mishkennet was probably not known to the widow who employed her; it was doubtful too if she knew anything about Sannie's family: how many of them there were, and what they did with themselves. Why should she have bothered with such details?

'Sannie!' the peremptory cry went up from her and from her daughters when they needed her. To answer that cry was the reason for her being there; no other.

Yes, they had sounded it always with that peculiar lengthening of the last syllable which had come back to Kobus across the teeming yet suddenly vacant years. 'San*nie*! San*nie*!'

That was all. There was nothing else to her. There was no relationship between himself and Sannie. When Kobus looked at her, when anybody looked at her, she promptly lowered her eyes. They were a sharp, dark brown, with clearly outlined and unmistakably black brows above. Sometimes, unexpectedly, Kobus became aware that she was scrutinising him or a member of the family; the instant she was detected doing so (or, more usually it seemed, just the instant before), her gaze went back to the ground, or to the task she was supposedly busy with. If he had been asked to describe her then (an unlikely request) he would have had to consider for a moment who exactly the questioner had in mind; then he might have said, 'Oh, her? A quiet little thing. Skinny. Quite ordinary.'

Which she was. But her fate was not ordinary, not at all: one last sad flicker of her fate being that he should sit at his desk, and stare out of the window, and lie in his bed at night, trying to coax out of the spectral past and out of the wreckage of what was left of his mind such tremors of recollection and recognition of her as might still be lurking there. Trying to know better why he should be haunted by the ghosts of children only she could have sent to him.

Sannie! Sannie!

But now no voice answered him, no form appeared before him. All he saw was the floor, or a blotched, aged, corded hand stretched out in front of him, or an empty street, or nothing at all.

That was his present life. He should not complain about it. Old and bewildered he may have been, enfeebled, overdue in keeping his appointment with the gentlemen of the burial society. But no one in the world, himself included, could doubt his reality. It was evident to everyone who saw him. Elisabet called him 'Master'. His son-in-law Shem looked mistrustfully at him when he made heretical remarks. His neighbour called him Mar Kobus, as a mark of respect, or sometimes even Rab Kobus, in tribute to his learning. He drank and he micturated. He ate and he defecated. These simple achievements were not to be sneered at. What ghost would not envy him them? There were places on the floor that sagged and sighed when he stepped on them, though his weight was now perhaps half of what it once had been. If he pinched the skin on the back of his hand, he felt pain; then he watched the little ridge of skin he had raised sink back reluctantly to the level of the rest, where there were brown spots among the hairs, hairs among the spots.

So real he was. When he finally died, he would have another life as a memory of some kind; a life intermittent and brief, in one sense, but also long. His grandchildren would remember him from time to time – as he had pointed out to them; if he could only hang on for a few more years, even his great-grandchildren, living in a world eighty years thence, a world unimaginable to him and yet doubtless much like it already was, would possibly have something to tell *their* great-grandchildren about him. They might even (who could say?) show them one of the books Kobus had printed, with his name on the title-page.

But his visitors? Those little holes in space, gaps in time, cobweb souls, bodies of air? They had come to him in their Christer garb, wearing pig-leather on their feet; she with a lace cap on her hair; he with a little red jerkin on his chest; ignorance written all over their faces.

The children Sannie had never lived to have; and their children; and perhaps the children of the children too. Generations never to be born.

Now he did remember something else about Sannie from that period, when he had supposed himself to be hardly aware of her existence.

She was the first woman – after his oblivious

infancy, he had to assume – whose bosom had ever pressed itself against his eager hand.

His hand did not hold or caress her breast. His fingers did not touch it. But he felt the softness of it nevertheless. Its warmth became his.

There must have been half-a-dozen of them seated at the table in the big room of the widow's house. Kobus's friend Malachi sat aside, looking on, smiling absently, keeping his silence, as he usually did. They were playing a game with a small wooden spinning-top of the kind you twirl into life with a flick of the thumb and forefinger. Around the neck of the top was an angular, six-sided collar, each segment of which had a number marked on it. When the top stopped spinning it fell against one of those segments, thus giving you the score for your throw.

What was done with this score, to what conclusion it was added up, Kobus could not later recall. But he saw the top spinning hypnotically before him on the table-top, its collar appearing to make a perfectly motionless, shadowy circle around it; he heard the faint hum of its point on the table-top. Now it slowed down and began to stagger drunkenly, before lurching over on one side, so revealing the circle that adorned it to have been nothing more than an optical illusion. In its place there was only a bald, unmoving piece of cardboard with numbers on it. Still the game went on, with the players laughing, urging each other on, applauding the successful throws – until between one throw and the next Kobus became aware of a slight, unfamiliar pressure against the back of his hand.

It was resting near the edge of the table, this hand of his. Glancing down he saw that Sannie was leaning forward, and that the source of the pressure was her little bosom resting against his hand. At once his whole body seemed to focus on just that part of himself: on the astonishing warmth and softness there. Soon his hand and the flesh which pressed against it were burning together. Never would he have imagined that something so soft could produce so fierce a heat; something so slight would have such power over him.

Sannie was not actually taking part in the game. In child-like fashion she was merely sharing in the excitement it had roused, and no one had taken it amiss that she should do so. She was kneeling on the floor and leaning forward to see what was happening.

With what result Kobus alone knew.

Was that child-like too? Was she conscious of it? He did not dare look directly at her, but again and again stole secret, sideways glances in her direction. Her face was in profile, a little behind his. Its expression was eager. Her mouth was open in a tense smile, but, hooked downwards in the middle, her fine, black brows were contracted into something like a frown. There went the

72

spinning-top; eager hands reached for it; more laughs and cries greeted the scores. Once or twice she laughed too, or sighed, and moved her body away; then, not daring to move, Kobus waited dry-mouthed for it to come back to the place (still burning) that longed for it. And what relief he felt, so like a renewed surge of excitement and gratitude, each time the pressure returned. And the wonder too; and the same, silent question as before. Was it possible that so tender a part of herself could lean against his hand without her entire body knowing of it? Especially when the shape of her bosom, the feeling of its being there, must have been almost as unfamiliar to her as it was to him?

The only thing he was sure about concerning this little event, if event it was, in which not a word or look was exchanged between them, and from which nothing emerged, was that it came to him as both a revelation and a promise. If that was what a woman's unacknowledged touch, an inclination of her body, a steady stillness of her bosom, could do to him, then think of what he still had to look forward to!

Well, he did finally 'become a man' (in one of the town's brothels) just a couple of years later; in due course he became a husband and lived faithfully (aside from an occasional, brief lapse) with his wife; he fathered his own children. Etcetera. But all those decades later, with Sannie's young breast so long since rotted away, uncherished, unsuckled, dishonoured, turned with the rest of her into the mud we walk on and air we breathe, Kobus would gladly have exchanged everything subsequently given to him later to return once more to the furtive incompleteness of that long-forgotten afternoon, and Sannie's small breast pressed forever against the back of his motionless hand.

Instead, the game broke up with the usual uproar, in the usual row between two or three of the widow's children, and that was the end of it.

Out of silence and emptiness, out of the cunning of apparent non-existence, there emerges another long-forgotten encounter. It was the first and last occasion that he and Sannie were alone together. It was also the day when the king of all Ashkenaz, Malik Tibnis, Tibnis the Shrewd as he was known, visited Klaggasdorf. That part of it, at least, the royal part, Kobus had never had any difficulty in remembering.

Tibnis had come to Klaggasdorf with a retinue of servants and officers of the highest rank, in the course of a royal progress he was making through his lands. In all, he had been able to make no fewer than three such jubilee journeys, at the appropriate seven-year intervals: so peaceful and prolonged was his reign. No one knew then that this was to be the last of them. By the following summer Tibnis was dead; the disastrous rains had begun; the time of the Ten Turmoils had begun.

Forebodings of such events were far from his mind or the minds of his subjects when he arrived in Klaggasdorf. It was a big day for the whole town; Kobus was never to see another like it. Only the sick and dying did not turn out to watch the proceedings. The marshal of the city, Bendor by name, with whom the king was to stay overnight, had donated half-a-dozen oxen to be roasted whole for public consumption; the Iriya contributed several kegs of beer and wine; all the schoolchildren were given a holiday, except for those who were to sing a specially composed hymn of welcome, to an accompaniment by the town band. The several religious dignitaries of the town had made up their differences (temporarily) and agreed on the order in which they would offer the various benedictions suitable to the occasion. Even some of the Christer notabilities, or what passed as such among them, had been invited to come forward, after the main reception on the steps of the Town House, to make a declaration of submission to the Malik and to express their gratification at his condescension in receiving them.

And that was not all, by any means. Merchants and mountebanks set up their stalls days before the king's arrival; a team of Muselmi tumblers and jugglers, from Taimon it was said, adorned in purple and silver blouses, did their tricks to the sound of drums and pipes; even a travelling menagerie turned up, with two lions in wheeled cages, and a manacled bear, and several monkeys in leather harness who pretended to pull the lions' cages, and tethered zebras and camels walking alongside. If you paid a groat or two you could go right up to the cages and touch the lions through the bars, from the back. Young Kobus was among those who paid his groat and was duly rewarded for having done so: he felt the stiff, dusty, yellow fur at his fingertips; he saw the flies swirling above it; he marvelled at the uselessness of the mighty club of the animal's paw, confined under the weight of its body in that narrow, wooden-barred cage.

And then there were the flags, and the soldiers, and the crowds lining the riverside for the first sight of the royal barge.

The Malik passed within a pace of Kobus, where he stood in the front row of the crowd, near the quay. For some reason Tibnis paused there to look around and to wave in response to the ragged cheers that greeted him. He was dressed in a loose white tunic of linen; his hair was curled; he wore a chain of gold which had jewels of different colours imprisoned inside its jealously swerving coils. He had a clear skin, and cheekbones that jutted out over his beard, and small, steady eyes. His eyes caught those of Kobus, and he said to him, unmistakably to him, 'What is your name, young man?'

The answer came at once, breathlessly. 'Kobus, sir.'

'And what is your trade?'

'I'm an apprentice, sir. I'm learning to be a printer and bookbinder.'

'Is your master satisfied with you?'

'I hope so, sir.'

'If he isn't, let him come and tell me.'

Was it a joke? It must have been. A moment later he had passed on. People swarmed on Kobus to ask what the king had said.

At no time during the rest of the Malik's brief stay in the town was Kobus again to be so close to him. But he remained convinced that day, and for many days afterwards, that the childish dreams he had secretly nourished of having been chosen for a special destiny were indeed going to be justified. Of all the people in the throng, he was the one whom the king had looked at, recognised, spoken to. It had to be for a reason. He knew Kobus better than he had ever dared to know himself.

When the reception to be given the king had been planned nobody had bargained for how hot the day was going to be. For about a week before his arrival the weather had been merely still and humid, with a diffuse yellow haze in the air; even the river's surface had seemed curiously quiescent, trembling where it stood rather than moving in one direction. On the day of the visit, however, the haze lifted and the sun revealed itself with a savage candour from a naked sky. By mid-morning you would have thought its burning rays could do no worse to those beneath it than it had already done. But there was no relenting as the day wore on. People fainted in the throng; the king himself cut short the proceedings at the Town House, much to the disappointment of those who had some special part to play in them; one of the men at work in the roasting-pits simply fell down where he was and died there.

Evening brought little relief. Warmer than an ordinary summer's day, the evening's darkness itself seemed misplaced, disordered. Voices and snatches of music rang out at random from all over town. Children who should have long been asleep rushed about everywhere. Flames pounced and clawed at one another in catlike fashion above the bonfires, and then fled into the dark. Altered in voice and demeanour from how they were at other times, strangers embraced like friends and acquaintances passed each other by without exchanging a word. Everything Kobus saw, the dust under his feet, each face he glimpsed, even the black, knobbly outreachings of branches overhead, seemed to him fraught with special meaning. A tumbler or two of free wine had done its work on him; so had the free pieces of meat he had bolted from scorched fingers; so had the uncanny warmth of the air; so had the knowledge that the king, the almost legendary creature of whom he had heard so much for so long, had suddenly become his interlocutor for a few moments and was even now, hours later, smelling the same smells as himself and hearing the same noises.

Surely he could not be wrong. Something he had long expected was at last about to begin.

As a child Kobus had many times undergone a shift in consciousness which was almost trance-like in its effect; it always happened involuntarily and without warning. He had never told anyone about it. Nor had he ever found a private name to give to the condition. At one moment everything in him and around him would be ordinary, just as it usually was; the next, he had been sundered, split in two, and stood at an inexplicable distance from himself. Only a husk was left behind; another husk stood apart and was aware of what had happened. The sound of his voice was like an echo from elsewhere; the sights that met his eye were remote apparitions merely; the objects in his hands, even his hands themselves, barely had a relation to him. One part of himself had been swooped on and carried away – whither, he did not know. From there, wherever it was, it could only wonder that the rest of him was still capable of moving, speaking, even remaining upright, and so hiding from others the transformation it had gone through.

The experience was always bewildering and frightening; but it was exciting too. Time passed in some different measure from before; the world went on at a distance; he remained trapped, akin to neither of the selves into which he had been torn. Then, with the same abruptness as the self-severance had taken place, it was over. Nothing could hasten or provoke its going; nor could he ever mark in his mind subsequently the moment when it had actually gone. All he knew was that he had rejoined himself; and that the world had rejoined itself to him. Back again! But from where?

In later years these episodes came more and more rarely, and finally not at all. He forgot about them. On that night, however, when the king came to Klaggasdorf, just such a spell fell on him again. He was on his own, looking over the river. Uneasy lights wriggled in it near the bank, just below the surface, like creatures incessantly struggling to move away and never able to do so. The sweet-sour smell of the water was in his nostrils. The sound of the festivities reverberated in his ears. Then it happened. The world shifted to a distance from him. He no longer inhabited himself. Turning, he was conscious of a remote, clumsy creature, which was also Kobus, turning in the dark. Near it, but far from him, stood a slender, bare-armed, white-bloused figure.

'Sannie,' said a voice which belonged to him, but to which he did not belong.

She turned, knowing nothing of the condition he was in. Her oval face was at once dark and pale; her eyes were only a quick glittering in the darkest place of all.

'It's you,' she said.

'Yes,' he lied, for that which spoke was not himself. Nor was it he who reached out and grasped her bare arm, just above the elbow, and felt the warmth and coolness there.

The figure swayed a little in surprise, then gently disengaged itself and disappeared into the darkness. Omnipotent and powerless, there and not-there, he followed her through the trees, over the uneven earth; both of them silent among the voices of unseen strangers calling, laughing, singing, muttering, arguing. Her slender form seemed to conceal from him and express for him all the strength and vulnerability of her sex; the otherness of her outcast and underling state, too.

He meant no harm to her, all the same. Nor did he do any.

She would not let him. She was too young and timid to surrender to the warmth of her own blood, the hunger in her heart. Yet he could feel from her how strong they both were and how she struggled to resist them.

And Kobus – ? Well, he was too kind. Too feeble, if you like. Too inexperienced. Too respectable, as well. He was incapable of forcing her to do what he wanted. It was not a fight he was looking for, no assault he wanted to make; he could hope only for an eager, effortless yielding of a kind he hardly dared to imagine, let alone manage to woo and win from her.

Overcome by the scent of her skin, by the quick touchings of her breath, he could do no more than hang on to a fistful of her hair as if his life depended on it. The shape and sensation of her body against his was different from any fantasies he might have had of a woman's body before: it was thinner, harder, more agile. She did yield – a little: she touched the back of his neck, she pressed herself momentarily against him and sighed almost sorrowfully at what they were both going through. Then she escaped from him again.

Eventually, still within earshot of the town, they sat side by side on the protruding root of a tree. The leaves above them, fingered by an inquisitive half-moon which had come up late, made a black but ensilvered canopy overhead. They sat no more than a few inches apart. Their hands sometimes met. All they did was talk. She told him about her family, about her baby brother in particular and the tricks he got up to; quietly, as if afraid that such an act of *lèse-majesté* might be overheard, she mimicked the voice and accent of the widow who employed her; she tried to show him, by the light of the leaf-fractured moon, where she had cut the diminutive ball of her thumb earlier that day, and solemnly explained to him what it would have meant if she had cut the soft ridge of skin that stretched between her thumb and forefinger. (Lockjaw, of course.) For his part, like the promising young man he wished her to think him, he responded with callow boasting about his exchange with the king; he told her about how rich he was one day going to become and what a fine place his home town was. Then they got up and walked back towards the town. They parted before they came to the first of its houses. She touched his lips with her own: so fleetingly, she was gone before he really knew what she had just done for him.

That was all that passed between them. Of religion, of Christers and God-Fearers, of her god and her people's worship of him, of curses and incantations, temptations and sexual initiations, magical powers and devilish pacts, she did not speak at all. It was farcical to think of her doing so: this grave, smiling, shy, chatty child, some years younger than himself, with whom he had sat on that thick outcrop of a root, his back against the trunk of the tree. (Remembering their meeting, Kobus was ready to swear that he could have gone straight to the very place if only he were taken back to Klaggasdorf; and the tree were still alive.) Within the limits of his limited character it was he who had tried to make something passionate and lawless out of their encounter; she was the one who had resisted and pacified him, who had given back to him his own boyishness. It was a gift that at the time he had been relieved as well as disappointed to receive from her.

Yet she was also the girl who, barely a few months later, would be accused of having committed devilish, vicious, shameful, fanatical deeds.

Lies, all of it! The only words put into her mouth which he recognised were his, not hers. He had not even said them to her, but to someone else, to his former friend, now become the accuser, Malachi.

The real pain of recollection, Kobus felt, remembering that evening, was that he knew all that had come afterwards. Everything.

Then, in the past, he had not even known what he would later remember – and when and in what circumstances he would remember it. So ignorant of the future had he been.

Of course he was now able to identify the ghostlings who were haunting him. Unspent possibilities, lives denied, stories never told, breaths never taken, souls forever houseless, hopes forgone: that was what they were: existing only in the perpetual present of what never was and never would be.

That was why they had come to him. Who else could they go to? Who else was there to recognise them? How much longer would he be there to receive them?

THREE

Malachi. The name alone, with its three light syllables, was enough to provoke Kobus into asking the question: Which Malachi, exactly? Kobus's friend? Kobus's enemy? The man who waited for a 'message' to come to him? The one to whom, at Sannie's expense, it eventually came? The public figure he subsequently made of himself; friend of the Lord of the Two Rivers; hammer of the Christer?

These were all one man, certainly, and there was plainly a continuity between each of them and whatever it then transformed itself into. But the continuity was of a kind that could be made out only retrospectively. Each time it manifested itself it did so by way of surprise and disruption, through a reversal of what had been expected rather than a confirmation of it. Afterwards Kobus was to feel that even the friendship between himself and Malachi of which he had been so proud at the time, and which he persisted later in trying to think of as having been with the 'real' or 'true' Malachi (thus, in his mind, turning the others into nothing more than imposters) – even this friendship must have been aberrant or suspect right from the start. Instead of being flattered by it, he should have been warned by Malachi's readiness to entertain it. Why had Malachi sought him out and made a friend of him, if not because he was too withdrawn and peculiar to make friends among his own kind?

In that case, could not something of the same sort perhaps be said about Kobus too?

Retrospective wisdom: the wisdom of the fool: the kind anyone and everyone is entitled to grab a share of. Which of course everyone does.

They were best friends, he and Malachi, for two or three years. A little older than Kobus, he was a student in the only academy of higher learning in the town. Traditionally there was supposed to be an enmity between the students of the college and the town's apprentices. The apprentices called the others snobs, ninnies, wet-legs, tom-cats: the last term referring not to their sexual prowess, which was said to be non-existent, but to the noises they made when they chanted their texts together. In return they called the apprentices earthlings, thickheads, hard-hands, and so forth. But while the apprentices shouted their insults for the whole street to hear, the students muttered theirs among themselves. They were afraid of what those hard hands might do to them.

All the same, Malachi and Kobus somehow

managed to find each other. Kobus could not remember how it happened, or when. For some
reason Malachi's eyes, with their enlarged, milky
whites, fell on him; flattered to be noticed by
someone older and of superior social status, Kobus
responded eagerly. He saw no danger in doing so.
He was vain enough to believe that he *was* different
from the other apprentices; it was only right that
the difference should have led to his being preferred
above the rest of them. The fact that the one who
had preferred him was so quiet and solitary by
temperament made it all the better; it gave a special
weight to his offer of friendship. At that time
Malachi was a thickset, watchful fellow, dark-
haired, thick-lipped, round-featured, a little shorter
than Kobus, slow to speak and to smile. When he
did bring himself to speak his voice had an almost
purring note to it, an extra vibration that sounded
from somewhere deep in his throat. Whether silent
or speaking, he had a habit of reaching out to touch
gently and adjust minutely whatever happened to
be in his reach – a book, a mug, a piece of paper,
even a stone or stick lying on the ground. The
mannerism would have seemed fidgety had not
each movement been made so deliberately, with
such careful glances and slight shiftings of his head
before and after, as if he were trying to establish an
ideal order out there, in the external world, as well
as in his own relationship to it.

Kobus was more than a little awed by him. Yet

when they were together he was the one who generally did the talking. Malachi contented himself with listening, staring away, smiling occasionally with a reluctant movement of his lips and of the skin around his eyes, while still seeming to search for something else his hands might put right. Kobus took full advantage of the licence thus given to him to hold forth, of course, and all the more so because of the respect he had for his friend. It was at him, no one else in Klaggasdorf, that remote, withdrawn Malachi smiled, and to him that he sometimes said, 'Go on,' or 'Yes?' (doubtfully) or 'Mm-mm' (less doubtfully). And when he said nothing at all, how could Kobus not think of that silence as a sign of acquiescence, even of deference? Malachi's sunken, unresponsive, yet always reflective silence, like that of a dark pool, was valued by Kobus more than explicit agreement from others. Agreement was banal in comparison, merely a concord of views; whereas silence enabled Kobus to fancy that his words were reaching a level in Malachi to which no one else had access.

And he was right (in a sense) about those words of his, as he was later to learn. What a fool he then felt himself to be: a fool in the past and a fool in his belated, self-reproachful enlightenment. Malachi remained as mysterious as he had been; but the mystery was at once darker and more lurid than anything Kobus had ever have been able to imagine. For by that time Malachi had found his tongue.

He came from a village not far from Klaggasdorf. His father was a well-to-do landholder, a freeholder, a man who owed no services to the marshal: someone of substance, in other words, who could easily afford to pay for his son's studies and for his board with the widow. Malachi was never apologetic for his good fortune in having a background of this kind. That was one of the things Kobus liked about him. Nor did he ever deny Kobus the right to envy him for it; for that too he won Kobus's admiration.

Their friendship was in some ways a simple one, while it lasted. Its small-town circumstances made it so. They used to walk about the town during their free time, or sit together by the riverside, sometimes with other boys, often on their own. Occasionally Malachi came to Hiram's house; more often Kobus would go to visit him at the widow's, where he shared a room with her two sons. It was a puzzle to Kobus how he managed to work in that noisy household. Only his gift for retreating into himself made it possible. The household uproar waxing and waning around him, he sat in his chair, a heavy book spread-out on the table in front of him, and swayed back and forth, muttering to himself, fingering the page or, for want of anything better, touching his own

89

cheeks or knees or the point of his thick, brief, curling beard.

But as for the stuff he studied . . .

The two young men were very different from one another in their attitudes and beliefs. That too was one of the oddities, or perhaps one of the sources, of their friendship. Malachi had to spend his days and nights studying the words and deeds of the Almighty, as well as all the details of the ways in which His people should go about their task of trying to please Him. Kobus's favourite subject, on the other hand, was the paucity (to put it politely) of the evidence for His very existence. With all the pride and conscientiousness of an adolescent heretic, Kobus pointed out that Malachi's God was invariably said to be kind, just, all-knowing, and so forth; propositions which the brute facts of the world daily did their best to show up as false or mutually contradictory. And if He did exist, but failed to prove Himself kind, just, and omniscient, why should we worship Him?

If Malachi enjoyed listening to Kobus – and apparently he did – it was not because he wished to explore such ways of thought for himself. Nothing of the kind. Kobus's words produced neither counter-argument nor anger. Just distant smiles, the usual fingerings of objects nearby, the usual silences and, 'You say so?' and 'Mm-mm,' and 'Go on.'

*

As a result Kobus had reason to envy not only Malachi's wealth and his status as a student, but also what he took to be the strength of his faith. That was precisely one of the reasons why he so often attacked it. It gave him the chance to patronise Malachi: an indispensable element in the friendship, all else considered. More than anything, perhaps, Kobus admired Malachi for his self-sufficiency; the fact that he so seldom seemed to be a trouble to himself, let alone to others. He made Kobus feel that being Malachi, silences and all, was not complicated and difficult but easy. Even being brave, in his own way and on his own terms, seemed easy to him. Young men, as Kobus uneasily knew from within, are chiefly afraid of being thought 'weak' or 'soft' or 'unmanly' by other young men. If the circumstances demand it, they will stifle their better natures, they will deny their own distaste or revulsion or even horror at what is done around them, in order not to appear weaker than the rest: whatever the rest may be up to. Any cruelty then becomes possible to them; little cruelties in some circumstances; great cruelties in others.

Malachi was not like that. He never went to watch any of the public executions or chastisement of criminals being administered in the centre of town. (Kobus had little stomach for them either; but Malachi never made feeble excuses for not going.) He did not abuse or persecute the Tsigani or Christer children to be seen in the street. Nor did

91

he join in the game the boys used to play with poor old Benoni the Simpleton, when they would gather outside his windowless little hut and set up a yell of 'Fire! Fire! Fire!' while at the same time holding closed the only door to it. Crazed with fear, moaning with fear, Benoni would shove and batter at the door from inside, until the boys chose their moment to jump aside. Then his momentum would send him hurtling out to fall at their feet. His white, bewhiskered belly showing through the gaps in his breeches, his face besmeared with snot and tears, he lay there, moaning still. 'Why are you crying, Benoni?' they would ask solicitously, smothering their giggles, 'What's the matter, Benoni? What fire, Benoni? There's no fire, Benoni.'

A stupid trick; but it worked every time.

The first of the transformations Malachi went through happened behind Kobus's back, as it were, while he was away from Klaggasdorf. By the time he returned Malachi was already estranged from what he had been; effectively lost to him.

Kobus had been summoned to Niedering because his father had fallen seriously ill. When he got there he found that all he could do was to watch the old man die.

Amos the Pedlar died both quickly and slowly; there seemed to his son no other way of describing it.

How many breaths does a man take in a day?

You can have no notion of the answer until every breath he takes is an effort for him. Then their number mounts up intolerably. And in a week — how many? And in a month? Each breath Amos managed to draw in seemed to give him just sufficient strength for the next; and so again; and yet again. He had never done anyone any harm in his life; he was just a pedlar, a man of no consequence; a kindly man in his way; ambitious for his son, if not for himself, so far as he was capable of understanding ambition. Now the harm he had refrained from doing to others was done to him by his own body, or by fate, or by God.

There was no help for him. Kobus sat by his bedside and held his hand sometimes. Illness had made the hand bloated; it was curiously soft and pale, as though air had been blown into it. Some of the wrinkles on the palm and on the back were smoothed out as a result. You can never know how familiar a man's hand is to you until you hold it in your own and miss from it certain wrinkles which you were not even aware you had expected to see there.

Kobus did his best to keep the surgeons away, with their instruments and their theories. A few weeks after he had returned to Niedering (a year it seemed) Amos the Pedlar died. His body was washed, wrapped in its graveclothes, put in the ground. Kobus was an orphan now. His mother had died long before; he hardly remembered her;

93

for the most part he had been brought up by a sister of his father's, a rather cold and distant woman. They said goodbye to each other emotionlessly, and he wondered if he would ever see her again. He did not care either way; but he grieved for his father, and in some ways and in some part of himself he never ceased to do so. He returned to Klaggasdorf. Hiram and his wife and others in the house expressed their sympathy. Kobus said the usual prayers at the usual times, believing in none of them. Then the whole business was done. He was a man. He had inherited nothing but Amos's paltry stock-in-trade – ribbons, rags, bows, buckles – which he sold before leaving Niedering to another pedlar; a man he had never seen before. He was the one would carry on a tradition which would never die: that of petty traders buying things from each other and selling them in public places to people even poorer than themselves. Kobus was to follow another calling.

The word 'betrayal' appears to have two almost contradictory meanings. You betray others by hiding your feelings and motives from them. You betray yourself by revealing against your own will the truth about your feelings and motives.

It was Malachi's gaze that first revealed to Kobus how he had altered. He would not look his friend in the eye. He could not do it. Kobus had been waiting with a special longing to tell Malachi what he had been through since they had last seen each other; in Malachi, he had thought, he would find a truly sympathetic audience for his account of those long days by his father's bedside. Anticipating that account, however fugitively, had been something that had actually helped him get through the whole experience.

But he did not manage to get far with his tale. He had barely, stumblingly, begun it, when Malachi cut him off. 'Yes . . . yes . . .' he said. 'It must have been difficult.' That was all. Except for one further, reluctant utterance, 'I wondered how you were going on.'

Kobus thought: Perhaps he's afraid of death. That's why he won't let me speak of it. Perhaps he's not so brave after all.

It made him feel sorry for Malachi. A weakness in him had been revealed. However, it soon became clear to Kobus that while he had been away Malachi's attitude towards him had undergone an inexplicable change. He did not come looking for him in Hiram's house. When they met in the street Malachi never had time for the exchange of more than a few abrupt words. Instead of sharing with Kobus, or at least seeming to share with him, those large areas of silence and remoteness special to him, he excluded Kobus from them, like a stranger, like everybody else. When Kobus next went to the widow's house he was met at the door by Malachi, who simply stood there, not giving an inch, as if to prevent anyone from pushing past him. He was busy, he said.

'When will we be able to meet?'

Malachi gave the visitor a slanting, laborious glance. The whites of his eyes, always prominent, looked thicker and heavier than before, as if some element inside them had curdled. He did not speak.

'When?'

'Oh, soon. Maybe, soon.'

He added mysteriously, after a long pause, 'When I've got my letter. Not before.'

Over the next days and weeks Kobus heard again and again about that letter – or 'message', as Malachi also called it – which he was expecting. It was always on the point of coming. He was reluctant to leave the house lest it should arrive while he was away. When he was there, in the house, he acquired the habit of starting up suddenly from whatever he was doing and hurrying to the front door, where he would wait about in half-embarrassed, half-defiant fashion, before returning with a lowered head to his place. When asked what this letter or message was, who it was coming from, why it was so important to him, he did not answer. Or he gave answers which made no sense.

'It'll be here soon. I know it's on its way. You'll see when it comes how important it is.'

In his voice there was a mixture of anxiety and self-assertion, of bewilderment and contempt for those who questioned him. His face and body looked curiously slack. Even his hands had become inert, except when he spoke of his letter; then he became agitated, positively tremulous; his eyes gleamed under their half-closed lids.

'Is it some family thing?'

'You'll see. Everyone will see. It will be important to the whole town when it comes.'

It took Kobus a long time to admit it to himself, but eventually the truth could not be denied. There was no letter on its way to him. The man had broken down. Kobus had lost his friend. He was recognisable as what he had always been and yet he was no longer the same. Who could tell, perhaps seeing Kobus so suddenly summoned away, on such a fateful errand, had tripped him into this particular form of mania. If so, his sufferings were even worse, Kobus thought, than those he himself had been through in Niedering. He had lost his father and had felt empty and bereaved as a result, as well as strangely angry on his father's behalf. But there was nothing secretive or shameful about such emotions; they could be spoken about to a friend — if one had a friend. Malachi's case was quite different. His solitude was morose and as inexplicable to himself as it was to others. But he had no wish to see it ended. On the contrary; he clung fiercely to it. The same was true of his constant state of expectation. He was enslaved by both. They were what he lived by. They were what he lived for.

He had become a sloven. That was one result of

the disorder in his mind. His hair and beard were especially dirty; they were full of grease; dull and shining with it. The attitude towards him of the other people in the house had altered; even more perhaps than either he or they knew. They left him out of consideration; they exchanged special glances with one another when he spoke; sometimes they teased him. 'Have you got your letter yet, Malachi?' they asked. 'Tomorrow we're all going to have a holiday – Malachi's letter is coming.' He sat there dully, not defending himself, smiling rather, with a stupid cunning and self-satisfaction, sure that his moment was to come; then they would be shown up for the fools they were.

Eventually he simply would not set foot out of the house, for fear the letter would arrive in his absence and be seized by others. ('The enemies who live here': that was how he referred to them, and it was obvious that he was not speaking only of the people who lived in the house.) The head of his school summoned him to explain his absence; he did not respond to the command. The teacher wrote to his parents. That too made no difference to him. When Kobus told him, helplessly enough, to 'pull himself together', he said, merely, 'You don't know what you're talking about. This message is for me, not for you.'

One of the games Malachi and Kobus used to play,

in the earliest and best times of their friendship, was to go to a rocky spot on the banks of the river, where the water sounded particularly loudly as it rushed by; there, facing each other, they would each step backwards one pace at a time while continuing to utter whatever trivial remarks occurred to them. At every pace they took they would have to raise their voices a little in order to make them carry against the uproar of the water. The object of the game, which was simple enough, was to see how far apart they could get while still continuing to hear what the other was saying. By the end they would be yelling their banalities at the tops of their voices; Malachi too, who otherwise was never known to raise his voice. The fun of the game lay as much in seeing each other's gesticulations and facial expressions as in trying to make out the words. Solemnly they told themselves that the game had a serious purpose: one day, when they had become public figures and leaders of men, the skill they had acquired in projecting their voices over great distances and loud interferences would prove invaluable to them.

Now it was the noise of Malachi's obsession which drowned out any hope of communication between them. How could this have happened? Whose fault was it? Where was the past they had shared?

Kobus used to cudgel his brains with questions like these. To no avail of course.

*

Eventually Kobus no longer went to see Malachi; perhaps, he had thought, though not with much hope, things would get better if he turned his back on him. One morning, however, as he was passing Malachi's house he was seized on by its owner, the widow. She insisted that he come inside; she had something to show him; something important; he had to see it. No, it could not wait. He must come now.

Once he was in the house, she eagerly led the way to the back of it. She was a thin, stooping creature; she had a weak, blinking gaze, a pointed nose, an inflamed chin and a moustache; all of which made her look a hundred years old to youthful Kobus. As she made her rapid way ahead of him, furtively turning her head this way and that, beckoning constantly to him, as if he might yet seize his chance and bolt from her, she told him that Malachi, at his own wish, had moved from the room he had shared with her sons; he had taken himself to a windowless, wooden den in the rear which had been used for the storage of kindling, barrels of cucumber and cabbage, and suchlike items. He had cleared out this hole, insisting he would be more comfortable there.

Now, opening the door with a dramatic gesture, she showed Kobus just how Malachi had gone about making himself comfortable. Around the wooden bunk on which he slept, scattered on the floor of the hutch-like cell, were hundreds of small, square pieces of paper which had been torn from the pages of books. The edges of every one of these pieces had been carefully blackened by flame all the way around. Then it had been discarded. It was obvious that the papers had been charred at the flame of the candle, which was the sole source of light in the place.

Many hours of patient toil must have gone into producing the mess Kobus was looking at. But what toil! To what end! As they stood at the door of the littered box which Malachi had made his own, the old woman brought her mouth close to Kobus's ear. 'There –' she whispered, half in fear, half-gleeful at having something so bizarre to show him. 'He's dangerous. He's crazy. Anyone would say so. I've looked through the door and I've seen him doing it. He sits there on the bed and he tears up the papers and he holds them to the flame –' and she held up her own hands to show Kobus how it was done.

He gestured to her that he knew already. He could see Malachi doing it: silently, with the utmost concentration, his eyes half-closed against the flame, the candle-smoke rising into his hair and beard, depositing its layer of fat there.

'What am I to do? He's going to set the house on fire! You're his friend. You must speak to him.'

'I'll speak to him.'

But Kobus felt he had nothing whatever to say to a man who spent his time in that fashion. The fact

101

that this man had been his best friend until a few weeks before made it even more difficult for him to imagine himself speaking to him, rebuking him, trying to win him over to behaving more rationally once again. And Malachi, this Malachi, would surely have nothing at all to say to him in response.

The widow leaned even closer to Kobus than before. He could feel not just her breath, but the movements of her lips against his ear. 'He's bewitched.'

Like a fool he answered, 'I think he is.'

He meant nothing more than that Malachi was distraught, half-crazy or worse; that he could probably understand as little of what was going on inside him as anyone else. That was all Kobus meant. But that was not how his words were to be taken.

'You see it too! Of course! Anyone can! He's possessed! We're in danger here. This is my house, my family, I must look after them . . .'

Kobus turned and left the house. He felt a curiously personal bitterness against Malachi; nothing less than a sense of betrayal. It was intolerable to his pride that the man who had picked him out and whom he had picked out to be his friend among all the others in Klaggasdorf, the man in whose silences he had seen a great depth, a profound moral fastidiousness – it was intolerable that this man should turn out to be one who spent hour after hour tearing pages from books (stolen presumably) into small square pieces; then pains-takingly scorching the edges of the pieces; then letting them fall on the floor in a litter around his bed. Kobus tried to imagine Malachi's state of mind as he did it; but he could not get his own mind past the picture of him in the act. By the light of that single, indispensable candle, Malachi sat on his bunk, obsessed by his bizarre pur-pose and yet wholly at the mercy of it: eyelids hanging low, the gleam of his eyeballs escaping beneath them, his mouth open, his hair besmeared by the fumes, his plump, thick-fingered, ever-restless hands, which had once been so tentative in their touchings and rearrangings, now working feverishly at the single task they had been given. Kobus saw all this; and smelled scorched paper everywhere.

It was horrible; not least because of its fanatical pointlessness, its footling pathos. Walking through streets sticky with the deposits of mud and other wastes, the autumn evening turning brown, black, green, blue, before his eyes, like an old bruise, only shrinking more, wincing more – who should Kobus see ahead of him in the street but Malachi, his friend or former friend? His back was turned to Kobus, his head was tilted to one side as he slouched along. Kobus wanted to go up to him, touch him on the shoulder, and ask, simply enough, as if he were involved in nothing more than an elaborate practical joke, 'Malachi, what's up with you? Why are you burning all those pieces of paper in your room?'

But he also wanted badly to go in the opposite direction and never see him again.

In the end Kobus did go up to him and tap him on the shoulder.

'Malachi, how are you?'

'Fine, fine,' he answered perfunctorily, not even turning his head to look at Kobus.

'You're not fine. There's something the matter. You're sick. I've looked inside your room.'

'So?'

'Those papers . . . I've seen those papers you've been tearing up and burning.'

Malachi showed no embarrassment at this. He still did not look at Kobus. He went on walking exactly as before.

'What are you doing? Malachi, you can tell me. I'm your friend.'

'No you're not. I have only one friend in the world. That's the one who's coming, the one who's bringing me my letter.'

'Oh, for God's sake – !'

'He's coming all right,' Malachi repeated. 'Then you'll all know what I've been waiting for.'

Kobus tried again. 'What's that got to do with you burning pieces of paper in your room?'

'You'll find out when the message comes.'

*

Nearly seventy years later it was Kobus's turn to find himself haunted. Daily he too expected visitors, messengers, presences whose comings and goings dominated his life. Was there, he asked himself, any great difference between writing words compulsively on paper, as he sometimes did, and tearing paper into a thousand pieces and blackening their edges, as Malachi had once done?

To each of us his own obsession. To each his expected visitants. Memories that rush on him like a wind through an open door, bringing with it seeds and broken leaves, smells of damp, smoke-smells, intimations of distances at once grand and futile.

On the street, all that time before, Kobus said to him, 'You should go home, back to your family. You need to be looked after. Maybe they'll be able to help you. You must wait until this – all this – whatever it is – passes over.'

Malachi was too contemptuous of Kobus and of what he had said even to glance in his direction. In his voice there was the same infernal, furtive self-assurance as before.

'I don't need help.'

Ahead of them stretched the muddy street and the shack-like dwellings on both sides of it; above them was a shapeless, many-surfaced sky; some lights showed in the distance from the market square. Before they reached the square Malachi veered off to the right and Kobus went with him.

More mud and cobbles; a trickle of water; a dog running by earnestly, unwearyingly, neck stretched forward, as if no other creature in the whole town knew with such certainty just where it wanted to go.

'If the message doesn't come soon – ' Malachi said, at last turning his head to look at Kobus, his lips mumbling over his words like someone sleeping, or someone waking '– if my letter doesn't come soon, then I'll know you were right.'

'What do you mean? Right about what?'

'That there is no God.'

They came to a halt. Neither of them spoke.

Malachi's shoulders moved up to his ears; his head drooped; he spoke as if to the mud at his feet. 'I should never have listened to you. Your messages have interfered with the ones that were meant for me. Talk, talk, talk – all you ever did was fill my head with your words. Nothing would stop you. Now I don't know what's going to happen.'

His self-assurance was gone; only anguish and confusion could be seen in his face.

'Every day I wait. The message doesn't come. Somebody's stopping it from coming. Someone is to blame.'

They resumed walking side by side. Suddenly Kobus felt liquid running swiftly out of his nose, like an uncontrollable catarrh. Only this stuff felt strangely light and thin. He put up his hand and

106

saw what was there. It was blood. There was a smear of it on the back of his hand, more between his fingers; drops were falling on his jacket, even on his boots. The splashes were black, yet even in the dim light they shone too.

Malachi had also seen them.

'You see,' he said, pointing at the stains on Kobus's clothes and hand. 'That's the message for *you.*'

With that he left. Kobus was to hear him speak again, many times. But those were the last words Malachi ever directed specifically at him.

A few days later Malachi was escorted out of town. His parents had dispatched one of their servants – a strapping, thick-necked fellow, all jaw and pitted cheeks – to bring him home. Kobus saw the two of them leave town: the servant carrying Malachi's trunk on his shoulder; Malachi, a full head shorter than his companion, following in passive, bewildered fashion, like a chastised child. The servant's strength, Kobus guessed, was a reason he had been chosen for the task; it would enable him to do more than merely carry that trunk, should the behaviour of his charge warrant it.

But Malachi went off tamely enough. The little procession of two passed within a few yards of where Kobus was standing: one dominating figure in front, the other docile, squinting, his head hanging down, a few paces behind. It had been raining all day; but as if to give them a mockingly cheerful send-off, the sun had come out for the first time. Its light flashed jubilantly from puddles in the road, from walls, roofs, the branches of trees; even Malachi's boots were encased in the silver of his own splashings. He did not see Kobus, who did not call out to him. Soon they disappeared into the dazzle. Kobus wondered if he would ever see his friend again. Conscious of loss, he was again reminded strangely of the death of his father, which was so recent and already seemed so distant from him. He was both relieved and grief-stricken; and beneath these feelings, empty. That was that. Done with. Over.

But it was not. Nothing of the kind.

Gossip and its best friend rumour got to work. Soon everyone in town knew that Malachi had been 'taken away'. Kobus, it was also known, had been a special friend of Malachi's. Therefore let him explain how and why the man had gone mad.

So he found himself a centre of attention; positively an authority in the matter. At first he was quite happy to oblige his questioners. Nor did he feel that he was being disloyal to Malachi in doing so; after all, had not Malachi been even more strikingly disloyal to *him*? When people asked him for his version of events he told them about the changes in Malachi's physical appearance; about the 'message' and 'letter' he had been eternally waiting for; about the torn, singed papers lying on the floor around his wretched bed . . .

Thus Kobus: holding forth, the man in the know. But he was soon to learn that his account of events was being confronted and disrupted by other accounts from people he was sure had never exchanged a word with Malachi. But they knew better than he did. They had heard all about it: in the market square, on the wharf, in the House of Prayer, all over the place.

Someone was to blame for the evil fate that had overtaken Malachi. That was what they knew and Kobus did not. Someone had done this thing to him. It had not happened by chance merely. He had been bewitched. Evil people had conspired with other evil people, and with forces greater than themselves, to torment Malachi into the state of frenzy which Kobus had described to them. That was why he had been burning those papers in his little cell, night after night, poor man. He had been trying to drive out of his house and out of his mind the devilish spirits that came there to torture him.

Kobus may have been, briefly, an authority; but he had always admitted to the doubt and bewilderment the whole affair had roused in him. Gossip and rumour, on the other hand, knew nothing of doubt and bewilderment. They were always sure of themselves. They always had new evidence to produce, new authorities to bring forward. Their allies were everywhere; and none, it transpired, were more important than the widow and her children.

Consider. There was Malachi, a man who had once been so quiet, so devout, so kind: now plainly unbalanced, mad, destroyed. In the same house lived Sannie, an attractive, adolescent Christer girl. What could have been more obvious? Who better to blame for what had happened to him? Who more likely to be the source of his misery?

Kobus never learned who had actually been the first to decide that Sannie in particular, and with her the entire Christer population of the town, were responsible for Malachi's miserable condition. He never knew whether the story had originated inside the widow's house and been spread abroad from there, or whether it had been suggested from outside to her and to her children, who had then enthusiastically taken it up. It made no difference, either way. Rumour had found what it had been looking for. Rumour soon produced an entire coven of females in the Christer community who were using their powers to corrupt the young men of Klaggasdorf. To achieve their ends (debauchery, apostasy, the overthrow of true religion, the destruction of lawful authority, the reign of the devil), they were prepared to use prayers, enchantments, bribes, the lure of their own lewd bodies. If the young men they approached resisted their offers, they called on occult powers in their command to punish them. They made them ill, they procured strange accidents to befall them, they drove them mad. Malachi, brave, suffering Malachi, was the living proof of it. All of it.

That's what rumour said. Malachi himself, being out of town, incommunicado on his father's farm, had nothing to say on his own behalf. His turn came later: after the outbreak of rioting in the town, and the arrest of Sannie and a few others.

The riot occurred at the end of the Sabbath, when a group of young men (apprentices mostly) set out for the Mishkennet. They had taken on themselves the solemn duty of wreaking revenge on the wicked Christer for the misfortune which had befallen Malachi. Also they intended so to terrify the Christer they would never dare to get up to such tricks again.

The noise of how they went about their task could be heard all over the town: screams, shouts, hatchet blows on stubborn wood, bursts of glass, the flat clatter of running feet. Then the smell of smoke.

The young men had left the market square quietly, with whispers; they came back singing, shouting, stamping, whistling, proud of what they had done.

One old Christer woman died during the riot; several people were injured; a dozen homes were looted; a house was set on fire. None of those

111

responsible were arrested. The following day, mild young Kobus along with many others went on a kind of patrol through the Mishkennet; not, as far as he was concerned, to intimidate the Christer still further, but simply out of curiosity, to see what the quarter looked like after such an event.

Surprisingly quiet he found it, less battered and changed by the violence than he had expected it to be. Like his companions he peered into the house which had been gutted by fire and abandoned (the black, penetrating smell of it seemed to him more dire and threatening, somehow, than anything that actually met his eye); he inspected splintered shutters and windows here and there; he examined the bloodstains on a set of cobbles. The Christer were all huddled indoors, which helped to give the area its curiously hushed air of calm, even of domesticity. The only real excitement came when a youngish, stout, high-coloured woman, capless, her hair and her dress disordered, her voice paper-thin, as if about to tear through itself at any moment and leave her quite dumb, rushed out of one of the houses. Apparently her fourteen-year-old son had been hit on the head the previous night and was lying unconscious inside. Now she screeched a challenge to the onlookers to attack her too, as they had attacked her son. Why not? Why didn't they kill her? What were they waiting for? When she picked up a big stone from the gutter there was a backward ripple of alarm as people tried to get away from her; but all she did with the stone was to offer it to this person and that as a weapon to be used against herself. 'Go on! Go on! Use it! Here, here's my head!' No one took up the offer; some of the spectators even began to laugh. So, stone in hand, she struck herself on the head with it, like a madwoman. Black blood at once appeared in her hair; red blood ran down her temple and cheek; then she staggered back into the house from which she had come. The door closed behind her. People stared at it, exchanged glances and remarks with one another, and went on with their tour.

Later that day Sannie and three other Christer girls were taken into custody. 'For their own protection', it was said, initially. Several more days passed; then Sannie alone was put on trial. She was charged with practising witchcraft, with trying to seduce Malachi from his faith, with inflicting cruel harm on him. The widow spoke up strongly against her. So did two of the widow's children, who had played with Sannie and been cared for by her. Other people, none of them of much standing in the community, soon came forward with tales of what they had seen and heard. Someone had seen Sannie and other Christer girls drawing squares in the dust, throwing stones into these squares, and then taking turns to jump on one leg from square to square: clearly the actions of people engaged in a sorcerous ritual of some kind. Another witness had heard Sannie and other girls singing Christer songs at inappropriate times. Sannie had been seen surreptitiously making the sign of the cross with her two forefingers as she passed the House of Prayer at the bottom of the street in which the widow lived. She had been heard muttering words in an unrecognisable language, an incantation presumably, when she met groups of young men in the street. Someone claimed she had seen her lift her skirt above her knees and make a gross gesture with her hindquarters behind the back of a learned man. And so on.

The public was not admitted to the courtroom. But word of what was going on inside it got out quickly enough, via the officials of the court and the witnesses. The latter were allowed to remain in the courtroom after they had given their evidence. Some people were suspected of putting themselves forward as witnesses precisely so that they could sit day after day on the precious bench-space reserved for them, and then carry the news to those less fortunate than themselves.

Kobus's own recollection of the courtroom was to be chiefly of the dirt-colour of its walls and its dry, rattish smell. Also the floorboards: how they sighed and gave up dust at every step he took. There was a bench at the far end for the two judges; also a desk for the note-taker, and further benches for the beadles, the witnesses and the accused. Next to the

114

accused sat the oldest of the beadles, nursing on his lap a cudgel supplied to him by a generous municipality. When the court adjourned each day, generally at about noon, he was the one who drove Sannie back to the lock-up. Five stone kennels in a row conveniently placed just behind the building, across a little paved yard: that was the accommodation provided for the town's criminals and suspects.

Picture Sannie in this setting: fifteen years old; clothed in a grey, checked dress of coarse cloth; her legs bare; clogs on her feet; her face unwashed; her hair clotted; as skinny, after three weeks' incarceration, as a stick-person; accused of barely comprehensible crimes; deprived of visits from her family (except when they succeeded in bribing the morose, cudgel-bearing beadle); no lawyer to defend her; not a friendly face in court; spending her nights in an airless, windowless, lightless cell; her casual words and actions transformed by the reports of others into supernaturally sinister and criminal antics; witnesses standing before her and reporting conversations which she knew she had never had with them and actions which she knew to be entirely innocent of ill-meaning – picture her thus and then try to feel something of the shock and bewilderment, the incredulities, dull doubts and night-time hours of fear she endured, day after day and night after night, until she must have been almost as mad and confused as Malachi himself, and yet,

115

unlike him, expecting no miraculous messengers to come to her aid. On the contrary: knowing that she was alone before a court which had found her guilty before her case had begun.

Then the trial went into recess. An official had been sent to Malachi's home with a summons for him to appear as a witness at the trial. It took a few days for the official to get there; then more days had to pass before he and Malachi returned. Not much more than a month had gone by since the latter's abject departure from the town, but he returned to it in very different style from that in which he had departed. His appearance was no neater than before and hardly any cleaner. He was still like a man in a dream. But he had regained something of his composure, and to it was added an element that was new. When his eyes opened to their full extent and he gazed directly at the people around him, it was not with fear or bewilderment, but with an air of condescension, even of contempt.

Then the gleam of self-pride and remote curiosity would fade from his gaze and his lids would indifferently, even demurely, be lowered again.

He was now a hero of a kind; a famous man; indispensable to a great public event. The messenger for whom he had been waiting had indeed finally come. What he would say from the public platform given to him would be listened to by everyone. How right he had been in all his

116

expectations! The crowd of idlers who hung about the courthouse applauded him whenever they saw him; some clapped him on the back and others timidly touched his hand, as if it had been endowed with healing powers. He was made welcome in the house of one of the two judges who were trying the case; he was visited there by the principal of the school who had written complainingly about him to his parents; when he appeared in public one of the beadles had to go ahead of him to clear the well-wishers out of his path.

Oh, the logic of it was plain enough. From a distance, and in retrospect, it would even be possible for someone like Kobus to tell himself he could perceive a certain inevitability to it all, given the circumstances of the case. (Though he had been incapable, of course, of ever prophesying such a turn of events.) Kobus was also sure that he was the only one in town who even noticed that in giving his evidence Malachi made no direct mention of Sannie. He did not speak of her having tried to seduce him or to convert him to the doctrines and practices of her evil Church. His eyes never once slid in her direction. Under questioning he spoke only, in confused and drawn-out fashion, of repeated attempts that had been made on his faith. Someone he did not name had tried repeatedly not so much to make a Christer of him as an atheist, a blasphemous God-denier.

To the judges and to public opinion outside the

court the distinction between these two heresies was neither here nor there. The one was to them as abhorrent and dangerous as the other. But to Kobus? *He* knew exactly which conversations Malachi, under the persistent questioning of the judges, was bemusedly remembering; he recognised the phrases Malachi haltingly produced for them, the 'proofs' against the existence of God he repeated, as if against his own will. They were Kobus's own: all his! He was the one who had argued with Malachi on these subjects, telling him why he could not believe that there was a God in heaven, and why it was far better for us to accept His absence, His non-being, than to try to conceive of an ominipotent and all-knowing deity who apparently delighted in our sufferings, or at the very least was indifferent to them; who had created cancers and scorpions, not to speak of savage and dishonest men; who gave us wills that went one way and passions which went the other; who filled us with rage at our own longings for virtues we could never have, leaving us forever entrapped in our doubleness; no better – worse, indeed – than the dumb animals we slaughtered for food and in whose skins we clothed ourselves.

And what about *their* sufferings: those creatures who could not even imagine Him, who had no words in which to address Him, but whose pain could be seen in their eyes and heard in their voices? We could at least upbraid Him for ignoring

118

us, or even, in a frenzy of illogic and self-contempt, simply for not being there. But them?

What an insult it must be to ourselves, that we should posit a Someone or a Something up in heaven who had the attributes of a personhood which resembled our own and who yet treated us as most of us would shrink from treating a dog. And (though this Kobus had obviously been no more able to say to Malachi than Malachi could say it to the court), as one more element of that insult, or as one more example of it, might be adduced the spectacle of self-righteous men tormenting an innocent child because the people she came from imagined their God differently from the rest of us. As if our God or her god or any god worthy of human worship could look down with approbation on such a spectacle, or any spectacle remotely like it.

No. No. No.

There was always a little crowd gathered in front of the courthouse while the trial went on: ten, twenty, perhaps thirty men and women drawn there, together with the inevitable, idle urchins, by the hope of hearing some item of news before anyone else did, or of seeing something they would otherwise have missed. The expectation of seeing paraded before them that which they detested, and which they knew to be weaker than themselves, evoked a kind of merriment in their hearts. It added savour to the food they ate. They sat on the broken steps in front of the little building or leaned against its walls; they bickered and gossiped among themselves; they bargained with the hawkers who came to offer them apples, pickled fish, plaited breads, even pairs of live chickens.

Suspended upside down, their scaly legs tied together, their eyes dull yet desperately suffused with blood, those chickens seemed to know exactly what their fate was going to be. Curious and hopeful dogs, too, went sniffing around the outskirts of the crowd, and occasionally fell suddenly on one another. Then there swirled this way and that a low, snarling vortex of legs, teeth, and furry, straining backs, while the humans fled – until an intrepid boot would catch one of the combatants square in the ribs and send it off yelping. But they always returned sooner or later, victors and losers alike, with all the expectancy and nosiness of which nothing will ever cure the race.

The court-watchers were a desultory, ragged lot; on the whole they were shunned by the more respectable townsfolk. Still, they served usefully enough as the eyes and ears of the rest. Throughout the trial there was an air of suppressed but unmistakable excitement abroad in the town. It showed itself in *sotto voce* conversations, exchanges of meaningful glances, sudden outbursts of laughter, even in an unusual emptiness and silence in the marketplace. The Christer lay low in their quarter;

they hardly dared to show themselves outside it. This in itself helped to empty the streets; it also did something to create the sense of an event, suspended strangely between the festive and the ominous, which involved the whole town and which would soon reach its climax.

Only two things made the crowd in front of the courthouse disperse. One was rain. The other was the close of each session around noon. Then the prisoner was led from the courthouse and hustled across the yard behind it. At that point everyone rushed to the back of the building in the hope of catching a glimpse of her. They had to be sharp about it, since the cells were so close and the exact moment when the proceedings ended was so difficult to gauge from outside. When they were lucky enough, however, they could raise a cry against the skimpy, huddled figure passing before them; they could try to reach it with their spittle, or even throw a stone or two. Then it was time for lunch.

This was the crowd through which Kobus was eventually ushered to join the select band of witnesses in the courtroom. Malachi was not the only one to whom a messenger bearing an express commandment from the court was sent. Quite late in the proceedings a beadle had come to Hiram's house, too. Everyone in the household looked on as he ceremoniously handed over to Kobus the folded document he was carrying.

Kobus studied it carefully. It did not give any indication as to who was responsible for summoning him to give evidence. But the official was much too grand to answer the young man's question on this point. He merely sighed, changed his weight from one bowed leg to another, pointed his important nose to the ground, and waited for Kobus to follow him.

FOUR

So it came about that Kobus was given a chance, a unique chance, to make something of his life.

Not that he saw it in those terms; not for a moment. He saw only danger in the summons he had received. Never a hope of salvation, of self-transformation. Never freedom.

His anxiety, panic even, when he appeared in the courtroom had a single source. It was the thought of his fellow citizens waiting for him, at best, to make a fool of himself; at worst, to expose himself to their scorn and hatred. He did not suspect them of cherishing any particular animosity towards him; nevertheless he was convinced that one careless word from him would have the effect of making the trial even more interesting and consequential to them than it already was. Then they would have a new object, an extra target, to focus their fear and hatred on. Sannie they might regard as an enemy from birth, by blood as it were; but Kobus the Apprentice? He could become one by revealing himself as a friend

123

of the Christer, a man who had chosen to betray his own people.

In other words, the person who had called for Kobus to give evidence at the trial was Sannie herself. She wanted him, as a well-behaved young man, a future pillar of the community, to tell the court what a good girl she was. She also wanted him to say that not only did he know her to be incapable of committing any of the evil actions alleged against her, but that in all the time Malachi had been Kobus's friend he had never expressed any special interest in her, or she in him.

Simple enough. Not too much to ask, she must have hoped (however doubtfully). She must also have felt Kobus to be under a special obligation to her in this regard, since she had so modestly protected herself from him on the night the king had come to town. (Protected him from himself too.) Perhaps she also believed – and saw no contradiction in doing so – that a secret tenderness and understanding had been silently established between the two of them many months before, when she had leant her small breast against the back of his motionless hand.

There were two judges on the bench. Seven decades later they appeared before Kobus with a remarkable clarity, the pair of them. He saw them occupy what was literally a bench: a single, wide, high-backed, high-armed, wooden seat. It was raised above the level of all the other chairs and tables in the room.

For all the people and furniture in it, the whole place in his recollection was no bigger than the downstairs room of his apartment in Niedering. A small, solitary window in one of the side-walls seemed to let in almost as much shadow as light. There was no other source of illumination. Sannie was seated in a corner. Because of the murkiness of the light, and the unkempt state of her hair, and the downward hang of her head, it was hard for Kobus to make out her features. He was conscious of other witnesses seated in two brief rows in front of him; most conscious of Malachi's round, curly head among them, with its back towards him. An official gestured at the first row of witnesses and they shifted unwillingly sideways to make space for the newcomer. The wood felt cool and smooth under his thighs and buttocks. The smell of the place filled his nostrils. No one spoke to him. At that stage he had still not been informed why he had been called or who had called him. He waited for instructions or questions. None was forthcoming. Everybody in the room was silent. He could hear someone sigh, swallow, shift his feet. Now someone else, he could not see who, was furtively scratching at himself: schurrk-schurrk-schurrk.

At last one of the judges speaks.

It is the boy, the younger one of the two, the follower (as he has always seemed to be) of his sister, who breaks the silence. She is at his side. Her hands are on the table before her. His are in his lap. They both look directly at Kobus. Their faces are the only clearly outlined objects in the room; they glow like soft lamps, alight from within.

In the high, self-assured voice of the child he is, the boy says to him, 'You are Kobus the Apprentice?'

That is how Kobus remembers it at the end of his lifetime. He is fully aware that this memory is errant, grotesque, utterly absurd. Yet that does not change his recollection of what took place in that courtroom in Klaggasdorf. He closes his eyes: the two children are in front of him, seated in their ancient double chair of dark wood. He opens his eyes to banish their image, compelling himself to return to the workaday room he has been living in ever since he sold his business and moved into town with his wife. He gazes around it, positively hoping he will see the two children there, reverted to the ghostly, trivial roles they have always adopted in his presence and which by now are so familiar to him: engaged in one of their incomprehensible games, perhaps, or staring out of the window, or conversing in silence with one another.

Nothing happens. The room remains empty of them. It is no longer their place. They inhabit that courtroom in Klaggasdorf which has probably long since been destroyed and which for Kobus himself has for seventy years been sunken into oblivion. Not merely do they inhabit it; assuming a role permitted to no child, they have taken charge there, they sit in judgement on him. They who have never spoken a word to him in all the visits they have made to his house, in all the different dresses and moods in which he has seen them, now address him gravely, formally, with a fearless attentiveness, using words that could not possibly come from the mouths of people so young. Their eyes do not leave him. He looks at the wall behind them, at miserable Sannie (no, not at her), at the floor, at the ceiling where random marks and smudges make up a map resembling that of one of the desert countries he will read about many years later. But he cannot escape the compulsion to meet again the children's unflinching stare, to expose himself once more to the heat and weight of their forthright gaze.

Nor is there any escape – not now; not then; not in any of the deserts he has lived in – from the abject lies and prevarications which come out of his mouth. He hears himself still uttering these lies.

His infantile judges, the children or grandchildren or great-grandchildren Sannie will never be allowed to have, hear them too. So does Sannie, who, having raised her head hopefully when her witness begins to speak, slowly lets it droop even lower than before.

*

How could he stand up for her? Who would believe him? How long would it be before the people in the court and outside it came to the conclusion that he was trying to protect Sannie only because she had already corrupted him, made of him her lover, her disciple and apostate? Should he declare publicly that on the night the Malik had graced the town with his presence, he, Kobus, or some simulacrum of him, had blunderingly tried to force himself on her and that she had repudiated him with more gentleness than he deserved? That she had sat with him in the dark and told him about the cleverness of her baby brother and the baby feats he got up to: his nonsense words, his wavings of his feet in the air, the dangers he would crawl into if he were permitted? And if he went on to describe the game with the spinning-top and how Sannie had leaned her little breast against the back of his hand while he played, and how he had silently prayed for her not to take it away, never to take it away – to whose credit, to whose shame, would the story redound? Of what would it speak: of her innocence or of his guilt?

These questions had only a single answer, as far as Kobus was concerned. Before him stretched his life and the opportunities he hoped would go with it: the career his father had planned for him and which he was eager to follow, the dignity he would derive from it, the respect he stood to earn from the people around him, the love which would be bestowed on him by the wife he had yet to find and the as-yet-unbegotten family he would one day nurture. In the other direction, the direction Sannie wanted him to take, lay only shame, derision, self-contempt. And worse: unthinkable suppositions about him and accusations against him by people he did not know but who would make it their business to know him.

What a choice! Who would not choose as he chose? How could anyone be expected to forsake the first path and take to the second – and for what? A little Christer skivvy, of all people; a girl whom he pitied, greatly pitied, but who meant nothing to him?

No, he says to them, to Sannie's never-to-be-begotten nurslings, I can tell you nothing about her.

No, I have never taken any notice of her.

No, I know nothing about her relations with Malachi.

No, I have never spoken more than a few words to her.

No, I have never been alone with her.

No, she has never tried to win me over to her beliefs.

No, she has never been given the opportunity to do so.

Yes, I did use the word 'bewitched' in speaking to the widow about Malachi's condition.

Yes, I am fully aware of the meaning of the word.

Yes, I have heard it said that the Christer people, their women especially, are skilled in witchcraft.

No, I don't know whether or not this is true. I have never thought about it.

The children listen without change of expression. At the end of the life whose hopes and promises Kobus had been so anxious to preserve, he tries to unsay with his tongue and to blot out of his mind his own craven utterances; he tries to banish the pair listening to them; he tells himself that they were never there, in the place to which his memory has now assigned them. They have never been anywhere; they are non-existents, creatures who were never called into being. (And whose fault is that? Not his, not his alone!) Through the shadowy chambers and corridors of memory, thronged with innumerable faces, shoulders, beards, eyes, expressions, gestures, he searches for a glimpse of the two judges who must have actually been seated on that double chair, like a pair of ancient twins: men who were so much older then than he was; who were even then perhaps as old as he is now. Men like that must have been occupying the place that was rightfully theirs. They must still be there, in some lost corner of his mind. Once found, they will do what he has failed to do unaided: they will drive the children out of the seat they have falsely and impudently assumed.

But no success comes to him. The clear, shining children's faces confront him still; unsullied by pain; unmarked by experience; clear-eyed, smooth-browed. Young though they are, they already know more about him, about everything he is revealing of himself and failing to reveal of Sannie, than the real judges ever did. They know also every last detail of what he will become, even to what he is now, today, an old man who sometimes walks up and down his room, sometimes scratches down random words on pieces of paper, sometimes lies on the floor and presses the palms of his hands to his eyes. As if that would help! As if that would make everything go black and impenetrable before him!

It is no excuse for what he did; but let this much be said of him anyhow. (He said it to himself, in his room.) He did not know then that shame, guilt and a sense of isolation are not so easily to be evaded. They have hidden pathways of their own through time; many crevices in which to hide; many means of returning to consciousness; much patience to wait their turn. Nor could he have guessed how many forms self-contempt could adopt, or a sense of futility, or the corroding awareness of failure.

But there it is. He could have behaved – no, not necessarily like a hero, not like a bigshot; but merely (let him now say!) like the man he had admired Malachi for seeming to be before his illness: someone who was self-sustained and independent, unapologetic, removed. Instead he chose what he imagined to be the safer and less painful way. He left it to another self, a later self, to discover, when it was much too late to matter to anyone other than himself, what it meant to build a life on rot and rubbish, the bones of an innocent child whom he knew to be innocent and made no effort to save.

There was something else Kobus could have confessed to the court had he had the courage to do so, though not a single question was put to him about it. Even the judges, those little judges, did not speak of it, nor did Malachi, sitting heavily on his bench, seeming to attend and not to attend to what was being said by his former friend. Kobus could have told the court that his was the voice which, in Malachi's bewildered recollections, had tried to woo him from his faith, to make his belief in God appear absurd and valueless. Poor Sannie had never had anything to do with it. Kobus the Apprentice, the reliable, open, conscientious fellow who never misbehaved in public and of whom Hiram the Bookbinder had so high an opinion – he was the one. The only one.

But of all that, not a word.

*

He hears the treble voices of his judges once again. The examination is resumed.

You are Kobus the Apprentice?

Yes, I am.

You are Kobus the Bookbinder?

Yes, I will be.

Why are you not telling the truth about Sannie?

Because it will not help her.

Is that the only reason?

Because I am afraid to do it.

Afraid of what?

Of what others will think of me.

You are not afraid of Sannie's thoughts?

Silence.

You are not afraid of what you are doing to her?

Silence.

Of what you are doing to yourself?

Silence.

You believe you will get away with it?

Others have got away with worse! Incomparably worse! They do it every day!

You are not others. You are Kobus. You will never be anyone else, no matter how long you live. This is the chance that is given only to you to discover what you might become, if you dared.

I know, damn you, I know it now. In some way I knew it even then.

But you hope you will forget all this?

Yes, I do. And I will succeed for longer than you may think possible.

But not for ever?
No.

Then it is Kobus's turn to ask questions of them.

Is that your judgement? That I should forget and not forget?

That is part of our judgement.

And the rest?

Never to become the person you might have been. Never to know how the man you might have been would feel about himself. Also, to be a runner-after the mob. A conniver in crime. A silent witness to persecution. An accomplice in murder. One of a multitude.

And you? Am I right about you? Tell me, you are the children or the grandchildren or the great-grandchildren Sannie will never live to have?

Look at her, Kobus. Look at her, Kobus, and judge for yourself.

Sannie's head hung lower. Her hands covered her eyes. The session came to an end. They led her away. Kobus left the courtroom. So did the other witnesses. People from the crowd outside came to him to ask what had happened during the morning's session. He made no answer to them. Even on that day, however, Malachi was the true centre of attention. He smiled faintly and yet reassuringly as he passed through the little throng, saying nothing.

134

He left it to others to give whatever report they wished on the day's proceedings.

Kobus walked into the woods, and did not return to Hiram's house until nightfall. The other apprentices looked expectantly at him as he entered. Hiram said nothing. Kobus said nothing.

That night, after Kobus had given his evidence in court, or failed to give it, Sannie used her sharp young teeth to bite open a vein in her wrist. Through the ragged wound her blood ran away.

At least, that was the story her jailer told. Some people claimed that he put out this version of the event in order to cover up his own carelessness in letting her have a knife with her food, or in letting her family smuggle a knife to her, which was what she had actually used for the deed. The exact circumstances hardly mattered, anyway. The fact remained that she had accomplished what she set out to do. That was how strong she had shown herself to be: strong enough to saw or gnaw through her own skin, through the layers of tissue beneath, to the last tough vessel which held her blood. She did not faint away at the pain she was inflicting on herself, or call at the last minute for help. Her blood spilled out on the floor: invisible to her, no doubt, in the darkness of the cell; warm at first; then colder.

When the jailer came to take her to the courtroom the next morning, she was no longer there to do his bidding. She had escaped him. She had eluded them all.

'One less to bother about.'

'At least she didn't live to breed others.'

'Bitch!'

The people who had spent days hanging around the courtroom were the ones who felt the greatest anger at what Sannie had done. They had been cheated of their prey. Worse, their prey had found the will and the means to cheat them.

Yet the savage remarks they made were never unaccompanied by guilt. It lurked in the corners of their eyes; it could be heard in their voices; seen in their gestures. The same was true of the fear their own words provoked in them: fear of reprisal, of having one day to suffer, or to see their children suffer, as their victim had done.

All the more reason, then, to feed their rage! To get their attack in first! To strike while their self-righteousness was still at its hottest inside them! The bitch had thought to spoil their fun, had she? To escape them?

They would see about that.

All day changing groups of people hung about in front of the courthouse and in the middle of the market square. Mostly they were made up of young men and boys, though there were some older, noisier, angrier males and females among them. Wandering from group to group went Malachi;

still the celebrity, still the victim, but becoming now, visibly, from moment to moment, a leader too.

The riot which broke out that night was bigger and went on for longer than the previous one. More men set out for the Christer quarter, they started more fires, looted more goods, killed several people. The next morning the first party of refugees could be seen making their way out of town – men, women, children, carts, goats, blankets, baskets. Now let them comfort themselves with the thought of the unimaginable time ahead when the god whom they they would not abandon would miraculously right all the wrongs supposedly done to them.

Within a few years many others, Kobus included, had followed the Christer down those same roads. The time of the Ten Turmoils had begun.

When the rains began some months later, in the spring, no one could have guessed for how long the blackness of swaggering cloud overhead, and the dimpled steel and pewter of water below, would be virtually the only colours to be seen. By the end of summer the tops of forests grew forlornly out of lakes never seen before or since; entire villages, even some small towns, along with the crops and cattle which had sustained them, had been drowned. Another two or three months passed before the water slowly started to retreat, leaving a landscape of mud and ruin behind it.

Famine duly followed.

Then came disease. Then the coldest and longest winter in living memory. Then invasion from the north by a nomad people who were called the Pessellim; a name given to them because of the small, stuffed, black-faced idols which their mounted warriors carried in their saddlebags. They raged through the country and departed as suddenly as they had come, leaving the people of the entire region to further civil and foreign wars which ended only with the eventual emergence of the Amar Yotam as their ruler.

His peace turned out to be even worse than other sovereigns' wars. In the end he and his men probably caused more deaths than even the plague had done.

The citizens of Klaggasdorf had long since done their worst by little Sannie and forgotten her; people further afield had never heard of her. Yet in Klaggasdorf and a thousand places like it, the community from which she came remained irresistibly available to take the blame for the distresses which tormented the region and the countries beyond. Again and again throughout the Turmoils, but especially during the reign of Yotam, a starving and bewildered people vented their rage against the accursed Christer; and were encouraged by those in authority to do so. No accusation was too out-landish to be laid against them. They schemed with the country's enemies, they concocted poxes and scurvies, fluxes and scabies, they stole children and ate them for meat or used them as proxies for the god they devoured in their acts of filthy worship. In their liturgies and rituals they rejoiced in the crimes they had committed against us; their uncouth manners and outlandish clothes were the outward sign of their megalomaniac claims about the eternal truths that had been vouchsafed to them, and the eternal servitude (at best) or eternal torture (at worst) promised to everyone else. And ceaselessly, in every way open to them, natural and supernatural, they schemed to bring that day closer.

The Second Coming, they called it.

This was the message which the Amar Yotam and the people closest to him never tired of repeat-ing. The Christer were to blame. They had always been to blame. If we ourselves, the God-Fearers, were at all to blame for what was happening to us, it was because we had allowed them to live and prosper among us. We had tried the patience of our God for too long. Now the time had come for us to carry out the sacred duty we owed Him. There was no middle path. No mercy could be shown to them. To show mercy to the agents of the devil was to act as the devil's ally. If we did not wipe them out, they would do it to us. We should never be fooled by the

thinness of their numbers, or by the apparent innocence of their women and children or of the menfolk whom we saw trying to carry out their humble
trades in our midst. Still less should we be deceived
by the fact that they were no more immune than we
were to the sufferings which the Turmoils had
brought on us.

They were dying from the same diseases as
ourselves, picking as we did for grains of rusted
corn in the fields, falling under the horses of the
invaders? So what? That was merely a sign of
their cunning, another fiendish twist of the plot
they had laid against us. If they were ready to
make such sacrifices of their own, what a sign that
was of how certain they felt of their ultimate
victory!

But God was not be mocked. Only when we had
got rid of them would He take us to His heart
again.

The people of Klaggasdorf saw far more of the
Amar Yotam in the flesh, while he lasted, than they
ever had of his predecessor, the Malik Tibnis. Or
even than they had of Bendor, their own marshal,
who had been one of the earliest victims of the
plague. Not for Yotam the solemn, seven-year,
jubilee progresses of the kind Tibnis had under-
taken. Yotam was constantly on the move across
the domains which, even during the relatively
settled spells of his period of rule, he could often

only shakily claim to be his. The Prince of the Two Rivers he called himself; but there were times when he ruled hardly more than an enclave between them.

He was a small man, surrounded by larger ones; he wore savage furs and soft leather; his beard was reddish in colour, flaring rather than fading to a triangular creamy patch just under his lower lip, like the blaze a fox might have beneath its jaw. Altogether he was animal-like: he stretched his neck this way and that, he was constantly on the *qui vive*, sniffing the air for enemies. In one respect, though, his appearance was wholly human, not animal at all: his eyes were pale, calm, unblinking, indifferent to others. Every time Kobus saw him he wondered: why *him*? What was it in him that made all the ruffianly lieutenants around him, many of them bigger, stronger, apparently no less brutal than he was, serve him so devotedly, and continue to do so through all the adversities he brought even on them, his own followers? Why were they all afraid of him?

It was no mystery to Kobus why everybody else, townsfolk, taxpayers, nobodies, people who hoped simply to keep out of harm's way, were afraid of Yotam. He was a killer. Kobus once heard him say, in a tone of sinister, boastful geniality, 'Even my shit smells of burnt fields!' – and none of those who heard him doubted that in his own mind he was telling the truth. He sniffed at his ordure, like an animal; and then made a metaphor of it, like a man.

Each time he came through Klaggasdorf he left behind him those whom his people had killed and injured; each time also he took with him dozens of men and boys, and some women too: conscripts, volunteers, camp followers. Off they went, sometimes to the sound of drums and fifes, sometimes silently, always leaving others to do the weeping. Then for a few months the town might enjoy what passed for peace in those days. But the Amar would return, or some group or another would rise in revolt against him, and the killing would begin again. All but the simplest forms of trade came to an end; farms were abandoned; wealthy men secreted valuables and merchandise of all kinds in places of supposed safety, where they were forgotten, or where they rotted, or from which they were looted.

Then he would come back, the vicious Amar, dressed in leather and furs, his muzzle whiter than ever, accompanied by his gangster army and the ever-changing band of cronies he kept close around him. Accompanied also by the one member of his entourage he had never abandoned or turned against: Kobus's ex-friend, Malachi; Sannie's supposed victim; chief hater and smeller-out of the Christer.

Of the two of them, Kobus and Malachi, it was the

latter who had, after all, become the success; he was now indeed the public figure and the orator that the two of them had once played at being on the noisy banks of the river. He was the one entrusted by the Amar to go nakedly among his people preaching his unvarying message. Malachi never referred to Sannie in talking to the people of Klaggasdorf; he never even spoke of his previous spell of residence there. Either he did not remember it or he did not care to remind others of it. On several occasions Kobus and Malachi stood a yard or two from each other and Malachi looked at his former friend, and looked through him, just as he did with everyone else. For him everywhere he went, every town he visited, appeared equally strange and equally familiar; so remote was he from his own past.

At a time when so many others had died or were still dying of hunger, Malachi had grown fat: another sign, surely, of the success he had enjoyed. The fat on him resembled a boy's rather than a man's: it started high on his shoulders and chest and simply went downwards and outwards from there, all the way, like a tabard. It made him look shorter than before; it also made his walk clumsy, effortful, as one swollen thigh hissed and struggled against the other at every stride he took. His thighs were like two obstinate men trying to get through a door at the same time. His hair and beard were still unkempt; his clothes were more dirty and neglected than before. In the corners of his milky eyes yellow stuff collected; sometimes it looked fresh and moist; sometimes hard, caked, days old.

But the conviction of the man! The passion! He was now the message-bearer, not the man awaiting one – with a vengeance! There was never a hint of doubt or puzzlement, never a trace of irony, in his voice; only a fatal urgency. The threats he uttered, and there were always threats in his throat, were directed almost as fiercely against his audience as they were against the Christer. It was the duty of everyone, men and women alike, to bring news to the Amar's men of any hidden groups of Christer whom they might come across in remote villages or in the recesses of the forests; they had to be vigilant to prevent any of them passing themselves off as what they were not. No excuses from those who failed in this duty would be accepted. No one should ever come to him pleading pity; or its first cousin, ignorance. Pity towards them! Ignorance of them? The presence of the Christer could not be missed or mistaken by any alert God-Fearer. They did not speak as we did; they had a distinctive smell; they carried themselves differently from the rest of us. He, Malachi, had been chosen by God, and by the Amar whom we were lucky enough to have as our ruler, to be our goad and their unmasker.

Not that he had always been so fortunate. Once, a long time ago, he had been like the rest of us:

144

good-hearted, simple-minded, disposed to think the best of all people, even of such people. But no longer. He had passed through a time of despair and confusion of which he could not speak, so terrible had it been. Now he had emerged from it to warn the Amar's people against the enemies in their midst. If people failed to pass on information of a Christer presence, it could only be because in their hearts they belonged to the Christer too. In that case they would be treated exactly as they deserved.

There he is in the marketplace, or in the pulpit of one of the Houses of Prayer, or outside an inn or a shop, or walking down some undistinguished street. He is ready to stop and talk to anyone, at any moment; in no time at all this or that individual will have grown into a little group; the group into a crowd. His voice is hoarse but vibrant; it carries even to the men or women standing at a distance from him. (Hadn't he and Kobus practised the trick of making it do so?) The stained and torn state of his clothing and the filth of his beard and fingernails show how sincere he is, how much he has given up for the people's sake. They listen to him intently, with an unfeigned attentiveness; they also know how dangerous it would be to appear indifferent to his message. So from time to time they interrupt him with cries of agreement, or with fierce, sagacious nods, or by telling him about their own achievements in the way of delating fugitive Christer. Then he embraces them, smiles, even weeps.

'A good man,' they say bravely (yet shiftily) after he has moved on. 'Such an honest man.' 'He knows what he's talking about.' 'Amazing.' 'Inspiring.' And so forth.

No one calls him Malachi the Madman. (That is how Kobus thinks of him in his heart, but the words never cross his lips.) No one reminds Malachi or anyone else of what he had been just a few years before: first, an inconspicuous student; then a freak and a source of scandal; then a noble, suffering victim. If others recall the episode, it is only as the first intimation they and he had received of the special role assigned to him by destiny.

About four years after the great flood, and well into the reign of Yotam, Hiram finally abandoned his house and business in Klaggasdorf and, together with his wife and children, took refuge with a brother of his. Since Kobus had always been the favourite among his apprentices, he took him with them: a stroke of great good fortune for the young man. This brother of Hiram's had a smallholding in the Gmut, which turned out to be not only an isolated but also a relatively peaceful part of the country. There both families managed to get by – penuriously, uncomfortably, always in fear that the dangers they had tried to flee would overtake them – but as well as any group of people could have hoped to during those times. Kobus worked hard for his keep: tending the animals, working the fields, collecting firewood, gathering nuts and mushrooms in the woods nearby, trapping birds and small game. There were times, he was convinced, when neither Hiram's family nor his brother's would have been able to manage without his help. Three of the infants from the families died while they were there; so did Hiram's sister-in-law. But the rest of them survived; not a small achievement as things went at that time. When the Amar Yotam met his end, and a grandson of Tibnis ascended to the throne, they returned to Klaggasdorf. There Hiram re-opened his business. Several years later Kobus married and took his wife with him back to Niedering.

So many Sannies passed before him in the days of Turmoil!

That is to say: so many innocent, suffering people, God-Fearers as well as Christer, from whose plight Kobus turned his eyes and his mind away, as he had to, if he was to survive.

But that is also to say: he may have been ending his days half-helpless and half-crazy, unable to command his left hand to lift a book or a cup, forgetful of what had happened to him the day before and obsessed by painful memories of more than seventy years previously. Yet he was not for a moment under the megalomaniac illusion that if he had behaved more courageously in the courtroom

147

in Klaggasdorf so long before, if he had used the chance given to him to tell the truth about Sannie as he knew it – that then the history of his part of the world would have taken in any important respect a different course from the one it actually followed. Nothing of the kind. The rains, the famine, the ice, the plagues, the invasions, the reign of that dreadful Amar and all the deeds he and his henchmen committed: over these events nobody in Klaggasdorf, Kobus least of all, had ever had any control whatever.

Nor would the best testimony he could have given on Sannie's behalf have made the slightest difference to her fate. They would never have let her go on the strength of his word. Her case had been judged before it began, and she would certainly have been found guilty. Her life was forfeit anyway. 'Thou shalt not suffer a witch to live.' It says so in the Law. And those people outside the courtroom looking for excitement (and those inside it too): they knew a sorceress when they saw one. Didn't they just!

Don't they always?

In more peaceful times Kobus was to tell elaborate but on the whole truthful yarns to all sorts of people about his ex-friend, Malachi. Then he stopped retelling his Malachi stories; mostly because he discovered, as time went by, that fewer and fewer people had ever heard of him.

Much the same was true of Malachi's master, the deadly Amar Yotam, Prince of the Two Rivers. So much for the fame he had once had. It had gone for ever, like the suffering he had inflicted on so many others.

Malachi simply disappeared from public knowledge after the ignominious death of his master. (Stabbed in the street – not by one of his henchmen, or by a political opponent, or by a maddened Christer, but by a husband he had wronged, of all people: that was how the Prince of the Two Rivers had met his end. Then his body had been wrapped up in a carpet and smuggled away by his followers, who hoped to keep the news of his death hidden until they had settled the succession among themselves.) Some said Malachi had subsequently raised a half-mad, ragtag army of his own which he had led southwards until they finally reached the sea, where they had hired boats to take them to the Holy Land. Others claimed that he had gone east on his own, to embrace the religion of the Muselmi. Others said that after the death of his beloved Amar he had simply chosen to live in a remote corner of the country, where he had remained unknown and solitary, like a hermit. Inevitably, there were also those who claimed that the wicked Christer had finally managed to get their revenge on him, once the Amar was no longer there to protect him. (Poison, stabbing, sorcery . . . There was no shortage of suggestions about the means they had used.) But his spirit lived on, such people insisted; it would never die.

No, the only story, the only life, which would have been unimaginably different had Kobus dared to speak up for little Sannie was his own.

That was what Kobus told himself at the very end of the life he had actually lived. He even went to the trouble of writing it down on one of the pieces of paper on which he had been scribbling his random thoughts, as if formally attesting to the truth of it.

But he was troubled by what he had written. He stared at it for a long time. Then he painstakingly added to what he had just put down the following words: If I had spoken up for her, Sannie's life too would have been different, in the little time that was left to her. She would have known that she had not been abandoned. How can I possibly measure what that might have meant to her?

FIVE

Elisabet had taken to chiding her master because he pushed aside the meagre portions of food she offered. 'You must eat, master!' she half-ordered, half-complained. But he shook his head. It had become an effort for him to swallow anything, even fluids of any kind. Tiny sips of water seemed to be as much as he could manage.

Also, the numb recalcitrance of his left arm and leg which had troubled him since his last fall had lately grown more marked. He felt it now affected the left side of his face too. There were regions of his body which no longer seemed wholly present to his consciousness. Or perhaps it was that they had gone ahead, leaving the rest to follow.

After their last grotesque appearance in the court-room – or rather in his memory of it – Kobus had expected the children simply to vanish from his life. It was as if they had finally overreached themselves. They had shown their hand. Their appearance in his recollection of Sannie's trial had been an *impropriety* (no other word would come to him) which must surely have finished them off. What better proof could he have had that they were nothings and nobodies who existed merely because his mind existed; in no other fashion and for no other reason? How else could they have managed to intrude into a memory that was so private to him it had been forgotten for many years?

Then let them be gone! They were no ghostlings, come to torment him from another, extant world, parallel to this one and overlapping with it, as he had begun more and more to fear. There was no such world. This was the only one we would ever inhabit. Everything they were, their comings, goings, starings, takings notice of him, ignorings of him, and all the rest, had only such reality as he had given them, no other. Did they indeed represent to him the children and grandchildren and great-grandchildren whom Sannie had never had? Yes, they did; but they could do so only because he had bestowed on them that identity; he had given them that form and the features to match.

The same went for their judgings of him, too.

They were his creatures; fragments of a broken brain, shapings of a terminal remorse; let them make no mistake about that. When he died, which he prayed would be soon, then not only they but also that damned mother or grandmother they had never had would die too; die again; die finally; and nothing would resurrect her this time.

Nothing. Not themselves; not Kobus; not the god/man she had presumably believed in, the world's all-time expert in resurrections and comings-again.

That was what Kobus told himself. Once again, though, he was outwitted.

True: the children no longer visited him in his house. It was as if they had been banished or had banished themselves from it. Now they lured him out, lured him on, into the streets, across fields, down lanes, along the banks of the tortuous streams which ran north and south of the little town. They did not let him rest. Again and again when he looked out of the window (and how could he not look out of the window, knowing what he might see?) they would be waiting for him, stretching out their hands to him, beseeching him with staring eyes and silent, open mouths to come to their aid. There was no sign now of the indifference, the blindness towards him, which he had previously been so puzzled and intimidated by, when they had been in the habit of entering his rooms as though they were the ones who belonged there and he the intruder. Now they looked out for him, they stared at him like waifs; like outcasts; homeless; in despair. And there was something else in their gaze that was even worse, that affected him more painfully when he saw it. It was bewilderment. They did not know what was expected of them now. They seemed to think he would be able to tell them.

Also, day by day their appearance became more and more neglected. Their clothes were getting threadbare; they were thinner than before; he saw them put their arms across their breasts to protect themselves from the cold wind of morning and evening. Their ankles looked especially frail to him, and their necks too. It was impossible for him to turn away from them, as he had once turned from Sannie. Once was enough. Even if they existed only in his own mind (as he had now proved to himself, over and over again) he had to respond to them.

But when he did go towards them they lured him on, lured him on, they led him further and further away from his home, beyond the limits of his own strength, until he could follow them no longer. Always they remained at a distance; yet whenever he saw them they were turned to him still, looking at him for help of some inconceivable kind; help which he could never get close enough to them to offer and which they would never have been able to receive. As he struggled towards them they constantly retreated; not like people, not with footsteps, not by taking paces he could see, but like a mist that lifts in one place and re-forms in another and yet always remains the same mist.

Except that there was never anything indefinite about them. They were always so clear, they could be seen so sharply, they waited for him still with their sorrowing, bewildered faces, in their worn, distinctive garb. Now here. Now there. Now where?

One evening he followed the children out of town, into the countryside, westwards, in the general direction of the big river whose waters would eventually pass Klaggasdorf. The elusive little figures ahead of him kept at first on a well-tended roadway; then they led him on to a track across the commonage. Repeatedly they turned to make sure he was following, they waited for him, beckoned him forward, waited again. Soon it would be dark. Could they not see how weak he was? Never had his coat felt heavier on his shoulders, his boots more lumplike on his feet. Suddenly he was overcome with such fatigue he could not go a pace further. There was nowhere to sit down – the grass was too wet and muddy – so he leaned his back against a stunted oak at the side of the path. The setting sun was grossly red in the midst of its carnival retinue of clouds; yet it tinged the flat fields, even Kobus's own mittened hands, with nothing more than a delicate golden light. On one side a group of houses, hovels rather, showed themselves as so many black shapes; the trees around them, also black, were less simple in outline. They seemed to come and go as he looked at them. Somewhere out of sight a dog barked and barked, each bark exactly the same as the last, forever incapable of becoming a word. With the entire sky at their disposal a flock of birds circled endlessly around a single field. The evening chill was already rising from the ground; its vapour invisible, its smell everywhere. The combination of space and silence, of light and approaching darkness, made Kobus feel that his heart would break. Surely he had reached the end now. He would never get back to Niedering.

The children were nowhere to be seen. They had left him at last; abandoned him there. But he spoke to them nevertheless. He told them how grieved he was at their desolate state. That he did not hope for their forgiveness. That he mourned not only their unlived lives, but the lives of all others like them; and his own unlived life too, the possibilities he had never taken advantage of. That he did not follow them in hope of achieving some kind of happy ending to their tale or his. The past could never be redeemed. Justice could never be done to it retrospectively. Its sorrows were never to be assuaged by anything which came afterwards. No belated fantasy could put it right. Its lineaments were fixed for ever in the grimace which time had given it to wear. Only oblivion, nothing else, could change it, mask it, smooth it away.

He was the one sinking into oblivion. It came to him as a sort of waking, a dropping out of the dream he had been living through, where the guilty were taken for innocents and the innocent for guilty. How was this? How could it be? What was his name? This place? Whose time?

It was quite dark. He was no longer leaning against the tree but sitting at its foot, on the muddy ground, shivering so much he could hardly hold his grip on the stick in his hand, let alone struggle to his feet.

When he got home he found Elisabet waiting for him, even though it was long past the usual hour for her to have left. She explained that she had seen him leave the house and that something about his appearance had made her anxious for him. That was why she had waited.

Exhausted, cold, weakened, dazzled by the light of the single, feeble lamp in the room, Kobus was much affected by the solicitude she showed. On the spur of the moment he told her that he had come to an important decision: he wanted her to move into the house as soon as she could, so that she could be there whenever he needed her.

How easy it was to make Elisabet happy! She was delighted at the request. She clapped her hands and did a little bent-kneed dance on the spot, skinny shanks and flat feet well forward, large bottom swinging to right and left. 'Oh master,' she said, showing him the entire length of her two teeth, and a great deal of dark gum above, 'I'm so happy today, so happy.'

Even in his exhausted state Kobus felt momentarily like a truly generous man, a benefactor to the human race. 'You see,' he said ironically, 'you see how we long for happy endings.'

'For me this is a *very* happy ending, master,' she assured him.

But it was not to be. Kobus spent some of the next few hours sitting at his desk and writing in the broken journal he had intermittently busied himself with for the past few months. The papers were found in a state of disorder on his desk, the pen on the uppermost page, just as he had thrown it down. Then, at some late hour of the night, or early hour of the morning, he went out once more.

What kind of old man's whim was it, people wondered, that had taken him out of his house at such an hour; that had led him so far out of town, only to leave him by the side of the main road to Klaggasdorf. There he was found by a pair of children from an encampment of tinkers, nomads, strangers, people from elsewhere, who happened to be in the neighbourhood. Neither the children nor their elders dared to disturb the body, lest they should run the risk later of being accused of having had a hand in the old man's death. So they sent a message to the town for the body to be fetched from the place where it had been found.

The two children were waiting there, as witnesses and guardians, when the party from town

158

arrived. Each of them was rewarded with a copper coin and told to go. Which they did: slowly, reluctantly, looking back, shading their eyes against the light of the morning sun, finally coming to a halt and watching as the cart turned and began lumbering back the way it had come.

A NOTE ON THE AUTHOR

A South African by birth, Dan Jacobson has made his home in England for many years. He is the author of several prizewinning novels and many short stories. He also writes criticism and poetry. He is the holder of a Chair in English at University College, London.